A Lake Thomas Romance

Finding Home

CANDY YORK

Cover design by 100 Covers (100covers.com)
Interior design by Formatted Books (formattedbooks.com)

Candy York
Visit my website at www.candyyork.com
and
Facebook at Candy York Author

Printed in the United States of America

First Printing: Jan 2019
Second edition: October 2020

ISBN: 9798690007942

For my husband, with all my love,
and for Lily, because you inspire me to be
the best version of me.

ONE

"Are we there yet, Mom?" They were the words Lorelei had been expecting for the past two hours. Frankly, it impressed her Beth had lasted this long without asking her.

"Next exit off the highway according to the GPS," she replied, glancing around to check on her daughter snuggled into a quilt in the back seat.

It was an exceptionally frigid March day by Virginia standards with a high temperature only reaching the teens because of the Polar Vortex, whatever the heck that was, Lorelei thought. It hadn't been the best day for moving out of their apartment, but they'd gotten it done, and all their furniture was in storage until they found a new home.

"Mom, wasn't that the exit?"

Crap! Lorelei realized she was so wrapped up in her thoughts she'd completely missed what the GPS was saying. "Sorry, Beth, I think we can take the next one and double back around," she promised, and sure enough, the GPS told them to drive another four miles and then sent them north on interstate 95.

"You're not too tired to be driving, are you?" Beth asked, sounding worried.

"No, I'm fine, just a lot on my mind, I guess," she said before turning back to the road.

It was still early evening but such a dark, cloudy night. Lorelei took the exit she had missed, and it got even gloomier because there was just no traffic on the road and no streetlights either. The way to Lake Thomas was not well-traveled in March, she realized, and the lakefront vacation homes would be mostly empty throughout the winter months. If it were like a ghost town, she hoped that meant she could quickly fulfill her promise in the morning and then move on.

"We're just going to drive into the town, check it out, and then we'll go back to one of those chain motels we saw on the highway and come back tomorrow," she told her daughter. When Beth didn't reply, Lorelei sneaked a quick look, and sure enough, her little girl had dozed off, which was hardly surprising as they had been up since before dawn.

In the split-second that she turned away from the road, it happened. One minute the quiet country road was empty, then suddenly it wasn't, and the deer was there, right there, and unavoidable. Beth woke with a start as the impact sent them into a seemingly endless skid that left them facing in the opposite direction on the minor road.

"Momma?"

Lorelei smiled over her shoulder at her daughter, who hadn't called her Momma since she was in kindergarten. "We're okay baby, I'm not sure about the car, or the deer, but we are fine!" Now, she was grateful that it was such a quiet road and thankful the deer hadn't run across the interstate in front of them instead.

Her car didn't seem so happy though as steam was hissing in frigid clouds from under its hood, and Lorelei knew she would have to investigate. She put on her hazard lights and left the headlights on too for good measure. She was sure there were safety flares in the trunk, but it was crammed full of moving boxes, and there was no way she could unpack all of that right now.

"Can we call Daniel, Mom?" Beth pleaded.

Lorelei grimaced and closed her eyes, saying nothing. "You forgot to charge your phone again?"

That was the crucial part; *again*. Lorelei knew she had an aversion to plugging in the stupid thing. Avoiding Malcolm much? A little voice in her head taunted. "Sorry, Beth, I got distracted today."

As always, her daughter came to her defense. "It's okay, the GPS says it's only a mile to the town anyway, we can walk that far."

Lorelei nodded, pulling her scarf up over her ears and her hat down as far as it would go as she prepared to face the bone-chilling air. The car thermometer said it was nineteen degrees outside, and she braced herself as she opened the door. The bitter wind hit her like a hard slap. "Oh my God," she muttered. "Stay in the car, Beth."

She walked to the front of her PT Cruiser and found a deer-sized dent that went about a foot into the hood. Something was leaking under the car, and she removed her gloves to touch it before it froze to the ground. It didn't smell like gas, she thought, but it was likely something important even if it wasn't flammable.

She saw the deer lying on the grass. It was huge and had beautiful antlers with a white patch across its head. Did that mean it was a buck? She didn't know, but its eyes were wide open, and she went a little closer to see if she could do anything to help it. Then, as quick as a flash, it thrashed its legs, found its footing, and ran off into the trees.

"Hey, we didn't kill the deer!" Lorelei called out and saw Beth grin, giving her two thumbs up.

She climbed back into the car and turned the key. By some miracle, it started, but it sounded terrible even to her untrained ears. She drove it onto the grass verge for safety, feeling the lurch of a buckled wheel. She didn't relish walking with Beth in the frigid air, but she had no other option. She sure as heck would not leave her daughter in the car alone, and it was getting colder by the minute. Then she saw the tiny little snowflakes. She usually tried not to swear in front of Beth, but she couldn't prevent a few choice words from slipping out.

"Mom!" Beth giggled.

"I'm sorry, but it's snowing," Lorelei bit out, trying to resist the urge to repeatedly bang her head on the steering wheel.

"Isn't it pretty?" Beth said, her eyes alight with the wonder of the winter's first real snowfall, and Lorelei couldn't help laughing. First, moving, then the deer, and now it was snowing, what next?

One more exit to go, Jefferson thought, leaning forward slightly to better see the clouds above. As his Grandpa Emerson would have said, there was a heap of snow up there tonight. He had spent his day at a real estate conference in DC. It had been informative, and he'd made some contacts for the law firm he ran with his brother, but it had left him with a killer headache that just wouldn't quit and run an hour late to boot.

He turned off at the exit for Lake Thomas and noticed a thin film of gritty snow coating the untreated road. It would get slippery out here real fast tonight if the predicted amount of snow fell, he thought. Since Lake Thomas was on the cusp of the highest predicted totals, they could get anywhere from six to twelve inches. Luckily, it was Sunday tomorrow, so he didn't have to go to work. It also meant clearing his driveway was not a huge priority; that was why he loved snow on the weekend.

He almost missed the little red PT Cruiser parked haphazardly off the road, but as soon as his brain registered it, he groaned. There was no way he could drive by the car without stopping, not in good conscience, and not on a night like this one. As it was, his leather driving gloves were barely keeping his hands warm in the car, with the heater on and all the windows closed.

He pulled over beside the vehicle and grabbed his flashlight from the console but found no one in the driver's seat. Drink bottles sat idle in the cup holders, one of them attached to a booster seat. The trunk was full of boxes. There was also a massive dent in the hood. He pressed the connect button on his cell phone in resignation. "Call Coop," he instructed.

"Hey little bro, are you staying in the city for the night?" Lucas Cooper asked as he answered.

"Are you on patrol tonight, or Artie?" Jefferson asked without preamble.

"Hi, how you doing? What's new with you?" his brother's voice dripped with sarcasm.

"There's a damaged PT off on the grass on Harris Road, with a big dent in the hood, windows still steamed. You know about that?" Jefferson asked.

"Damn, no, I'll check it out. I was out there about an hour ago, and the road was clear. Look out for the driver as you come up," Lucas Cooper, Coop to his friends and family, switched instantly to sheriff mode.

"There might be a passenger too, a child; there's a booster seat."

"Geez, this is no night for a kid to be out," Coop muttered.

Jefferson agreed before he hung up and set off toward town. Judging by the steamy windows, and the fact his brother had been out this way recently, the driver and passenger should have had time to make it to town. But, his gut was telling him differently.

He saw the swinging of a small light up ahead, and, as he got closer, he realized it belonged to a flashlight held by two children walking hand in hand in the grass beside the road. They had to be from the PT, but where was the driver? He wondered. They didn't immediately turn around, but when he pulled over just ahead of them, they stopped dead in their snowy tracks. He got out of his SUV, amazed at how cold it had gotten since he had left the conference and how much the tiny chips of icy snow stung his face. "Do you two need a ride to town?"

They looked at each other, and the smaller one leaned in closer, and then the bigger one spoke. "We're fine, thank you."

He was about to open his rear passenger door when his brain registered the refusal and the tone of its delivery. His sister, Grace, always used that tone when he annoyed her. The bigger one was a woman, he thought, no doubt, she was the driver.

"Listen, ma'am, it's cold out here, and the snow will come down harder any minute. I'm just offering you a ride, that's all," he didn't mean to be so abrupt or to sound like a jerk, but his head was pounding, and it was cold enough to freeze the nuts off a squirrel. He just wanted to get home.

"Well, since you offered so nicely," the woman responded in a voice that could rival the air temperature for iciness. "No, thank you!"

He rubbed his forehead. "Look, lady, I have a headache, I'm not an ax murderer or a serial killer. I'm just a lawyer. My name is Jefferson, I have a small practice in Lake Thomas, and I can't leave you out here in the cold."

The woman and child kept walking, going right by his car, heading for town.

"Are you kidding me?" He called after them incredulously. "You'd rather freeze?"

Lorelei smiled when she saw another vehicle coming, but as soon as the man got out of it, her relief turned to unease. He had to be well over six feet. She could see his face over the roof of his SUV. When he walked over to them, Beth edged closer to her. He was wearing a long, dark overcoat and a thick scarf but no hat. His hair was as black as the night sky had been before it filled with clouds. He wasn't doing anything threatening and yet she still felt intimidated by the sheer size of him.

He also hadn't liked it when she had said no. His attitude reminded her they were alone on a two-lane road, basically in the middle of nowhere, and neither of them was up to a run. She kept walking, and Beth kept up, even though Lorelei was sure she could hear a faint wheezing noise. "Keep your head down, Beth, try to breathe through your scarf."

"Yes, Momma."

Twice in one evening, Lorelei thought. Her daughter was afraid and trying hard not to show it. A glance over her shoulder told Lorelei what she already suspected; the SUV was cruising along at about two miles an hour, right behind them. The driver must have decided that if she wouldn't get in his vehicle, he would simply escort them.

She stopped walking and looked right at him through his windshield. Although she'd swathed most of her face in her scarf, she knew he could see her. "Look, mister, we don't want or need your help."

He looked as if he would have stopped his car and gotten out, and he seemed irritated as hell until she saw his eyes switch ahead and his scowl lessened. Lorelei saw more headlights approaching and felt slightly relieved. What were the chances two serial killers were working together in one small town? She thought.

As the vehicle got closer, she realized it had a bar of lights on the roof and the front grill. The sirens wailed, and the lights came on as the officer pulled onto the grass and did a U-turn before he stopped beside them. He got out, putting on his hat and zipping his jacket up to his neck.

"He's wearing a cowboy hat," Beth whispered.

Lorelei knew it wasn't a cowboy hat, but mostly she was wondering what they fed the men in this town because this guy had to be at least six feet tall too.

"Evening ma'am, Sheriff Cooper, I hear you had a problem with your vehicle," he said, tipping his hat but not removing it.

"We hit a deer. It was a massive one. Mom thinks it killed our car, but the deer was okay. It ran away!" Beth said in a rush, the words a little muffled by the scarf wrapped around her face.

"You're both okay?" The sheriff asked, smiling as he addressed them.

"We are," Lorelei answered. The sheriff knew something damaged her car, she realized, which meant Mr. Congeniality must have called him when he saw it. It also told her the guy was not so bad, and she added 'apologize to a total stranger' to her lengthy to-do list.

"Let's get you both into my vehicle and get you to town. You can get something to eat and warm up, and we can call for a tow. Most places are closing up, but I know the diner is staying open late tonight for the plow drivers," the sheriff said.

Lorelei and Beth walked over and got into the back seat of the sheriff's SUV. It felt toasty warm, and the air inside was more comfortable to breathe. Beth snuggled in close to her, and she wrapped her arm around her daughter's shoulders. "It's all going to be fine now," she said, and for some unfathomable reason, she knew it would be.

Jefferson looked at his brother, who was smirking in that annoying way brothers had. "Don't start with me!" he warned.

"I wouldn't dream of it, little brother," Lucas said, laughing as he walked back and got into the driver's seat.

Coop found it so amusing he hadn't been able to get the woman or her daughter into his car, Jefferson thought, despite the bitterly chilly temperature. He knew his attitude had a lot to do with that, but hell, this was one stubborn woman. Stranger danger was one thing in the city, but Lake Thomas was small. People in the town helped each other out. Why did a simple offer of help cause her hackles to rise? He wondered.

He followed his brother into town and pulled into King Toby's parking lot, two spaces over. He needed a coffee and something to eat to dull his headache, and, if he were honest, he wanted to check on the child. He guessed it was probably a girl under all those layers, and he'd heard the concern in her mother's voice.

Toby's place was as warm and inviting as ever. The older man greeted them with a beaming smile and a loud hello. Jefferson watched in amazement as the woman smiled in return. At the same time, she removed multiple layers from herself and her daughter. The child had thick blond hair hanging in a messy braid halfway down her back. She looked a little pale and tired and was occasionally coughing. He glanced across at the woman as she removed a weird looped scarf from around her neck and head and shrugged out of a thick beanie. Her hair was crazy with static from the hat, and it was wildly curly. It was golden blond, just like her daughter's, but only reached her shoulders. She regarded him coldly for a few seconds, and he looked away, but not before he'd glimpsed the bluest pair of eyes he'd ever seen in his life.

Lorelei shrugged out of her coat and hung it on the hook at the end of the booth. She reached into her backpack and took out a plastic zipper bag containing Beth's asthma inhaler and spacer. Beth looked at it despondently before giving in. She hated using it because some kids made fun of her, but there were no kids in the restaurant, and Lorelei knew she needed it.

He was looking over at their booth again, watching Beth use the inhaler. When Beth caught him looking, Lorelei saw her daughter square her shoulders immediately. "That works in minutes for my sister, Grace. You'll be feeling better in no time," he said kindly, making Lorelei feel even more guilty about not trusting him.

He looked at her then, and she could see he was weighing his words, so she decided it was as good a time as any to tick one item off her never-ending list. "I'm sorry I wouldn't get in your car before. I should have, I know that now, but I think I've seen one too many Dateline specials."

He almost smiled, lines of fatigue etched around his mouth, his expression softening. His eyes were a dark, slate gray, Lorelei realized, and he wasn't too scary when he was sitting down. He was looking back at her, and she knew it was because she was staring at him and not saying anything. "Sorry, spaced out there for a moment. It's been an endless day."

"Try Toby's special coffee. It tastes like diesel oil, but it could wake the dead," the sheriff said as he walked over to their booth. "So, what made you drive out to Lake Thomas on a day like today?"

"I didn't realize the weather would be so bad," she admitted. "We were moving, and I didn't check the forecast yesterday. Lesson learned!"

"Tough day," the sheriff said succinctly, making Lorelei smile. "So, you're moving into town?"

Lorelei wasn't sure if there was a law against scattering her friend's ashes on public land. Still, considering the day she'd had, she wasn't willing to risk telling the sheriff why she was really in town. It seemed everyone was waiting for her to answer, including Beth, who looked confused.

"We got off the highway at the wrong exit, and before we could make a U-turn, the deer ran right in front of us," she said. Beth didn't contradict her, just gave her a curious look. Her guilt meter kicked in about lying to the sheriff, but life had been giving her lemons for a while, and she wasn't ready to risk making any lemonade just yet.

"Looks like you ladies are stuck here then," said another voice, and Lorelei saw an elderly man walking over to them. "I'm Toby King," the man offered his hand to Beth. "What's your name, little lady?"

"Beth Hannah and this is my Mom, Lorelei M-," Beth jumped at the quick jab of Lorelei's foot under the table.

Standing up, she offered her hand to Toby. "Lorelei Hannah," she said.

"Ah, such a beautiful name," Toby said in a lilting voice, flirting outrageously, Lorelei realized. He had to be over seventy, his thick hair was pure white, and he used a cane to walk, but he was at least one male in this town under six feet, and he had a twinkle in his eyes that made her want to smile. "Do you need to call someone, let them know what happened?"

Lorelei shook her head. There was only one person she might call, her friend Daniel, but there was no need to call him tonight. Tomorrow was soon enough.

Jefferson watched Toby flirt with the woman he hadn't even been able to convince to get into his SUV. He knew it was ridiculous, but he felt a tiny spurt of jealousy at the older man's amiable nature. "I'm off," he snapped, turning for the door but not before his brother shot him an incredulous glare that stopped him dead. "It's been a long day," he said, turning to walk out of the door and over to his Explorer in the parking lot.

"What the hell was that about?" Coop caught up with him as he climbed into the driver's seat.

"Sorry, headache, just want to get home," He replied, not entirely lying since his head was pounding like a jackhammer.

"I could use an extra plow driver tonight," Coop said.

"What about Jackson?"

Lucas Cooper squared his shoulders and walked up to the window. "I already asked him, and he's in, but we have two of our regular volunteers out sick with the flu."

There was no way out, Jefferson realized. "Fine, I'm in, but I have to change, this is an expensive suit." He also planned on swallowing some Tylenol before venturing out into the cold again.

"Okay, Mr. Big Shot lawyer, change the suit," Coop laughed. "We're meeting back at Toby's around ten, we'll see you then."

Jefferson watched his brother go back into the diner in his rearview mirror as he drove the half-mile down Main Street before turning off down the dirt road to his small ranch home. Only about an inch of snow was coating the unpaved road so far, but it was falling fast and furious.

He still fondly remembered his time living in Washington, DC, and how the plows would wake him up during the night as the drivers cleared the snow emergency lanes. It was only on days like this he missed living in the city. It would be one long, snowy night of plowing.

Lorelei was on her third cup of coffee when Earl, the tow truck guy, drove by with her mangled PT on his way to his lot off Main Street. The snow was coming down now, and the wind had picked up. Beth was curled up on the booth seat opposite, watching a movie on her tablet and struggling hard to keep her eyes open even though it was only a little after nine.

Sheriff Cooper had been in and out for the past hour. Volunteers kept showing up to help plow the predicted snowfall. The restaurant owner, Toby King, happily served up pancakes, eggs, and pie to everyone. Lorelei had never seen anything quite like how Lake Thomas was rallying around to make sure its streets were safe. There was a feeling of community about the place she'd never experienced before, and it felt welcoming.

It made her feel more than a little guilty that she'd been so distrustful of Jefferson when he'd offered to help them. Still, she had Beth to consider, and the whole issue with Malcolm, her soon-to-be ex, had just made her wary of men and with good reason. Ugh, why was everything in her life such a mess? She thought bitterly.

"How are you ladies doing?"

Lorelei looked around and found Toby approaching the booth again.

"As good as we can be, considering the day we've had," Lorelei answered honestly.

"Well, I have grand news, I hope," the old man began. "I rent out some places in the summer, but not at this time of year. They're right across the street, and you're welcome to stay in one until the storm passes."

"Seriously?" Lorelei asked. Thanks to Toby's offer, they would have a place to stay while she sorted out the whole car nightmare. "How much?" She crossed her fingers, praying her bank account wouldn't take too much of a hit.

"How much?" Toby laughed. "My dear lady, you can stay there for free. I don't rent them out in winter, especially in the middle of a snowstorm, but I do always have the heat on to protect the pipes from a freeze."

Was he kidding? Lorelei thought, but one look at the man's face assured her he was not, and she felt tears welling up in her eyes. "I don't know what to say, except thank you."

"We all need a lucky break sometime," Toby said. "I'll get you a key and have one of the guys walk you over before the snow gets any worse, and you get stuck camping out in my diner!"

True to his word, he returned with a set of keys and the sheriff about fifteen minutes later. Lorelei got Beth ready to brave the chilly air for the quick walk to the other side of Main Street.

It was as if karma was turning around on them and finally giving them some good luck, she thought. They gathered their belongings and were just heading out the front door, when Beth turned around and ran back to Toby and hugged him, then ran back to the door. Lorelei smiled, turning to leave and saw Sheriff Cooper talking to more snowplow recruits, one of whom she realized was his brother, Jefferson. They both nodded, and the latter even managed a half-hearted smile for Beth before he went into the diner.

The other volunteer laughed. "Our brother, the anti-social one!" he commented drily. "Jackson Cooper, at your service, ladies, welcome to town."

Lorelei couldn't help smiling. Brothers? That explained how they were all so tall. It was genetic. "Thanks. Nice to meet you, Jackson."

"Okay, time to get across the street before this little one falls asleep standing up," the sheriff said, and, with no effort at all, he scooped Beth up and strode across the street. Lorelei looked back over her shoulder at the diner one more time and was sure she saw Jefferson Cooper watching them. Then, she followed the sheriff across the street through the crisp snow. Tomorrow, she would figure out what happened next, but for tonight she planned on going with the flow, especially if that included a soft, warm bed to sleep in!

TWO

Lorelei woke up groggily the next morning, trying to figure out how daylight was coming through the blind slats on the window when she didn't have shades in her bedroom. She sat up in a strange bed, and everything came rushing back to her. Her car was most likely totaled, the tow truck driver had said. She'd called her insurance company and reported the accident. Still, they wouldn't be able to do anything for a few days because of the weather.

Now, she was staying in a summer rental unit in Lake Thomas in the middle of a snowstorm that had dumped about six inches of snow before she'd crawled into bed in the wee hours. She couldn't help counting her blessings. What a difference a day could make, she thought.

She slid out from under the covers slowly so as not to disturb Beth. The moment her feet hit the hardwood floor, she felt the chill and scurried across to the chair where she'd dumped her clothes. She pulled her sweater over her head, grabbed her socks from the day before, and then padded over to the window in the living room. The sight that met her eyes when she pulled open the curtains was incredible. What last night had been around half a foot of snow was now at least double that, and in some places, the wind had caused it to drift much higher.

Someone had been by not that long ago to plow again, and Lorelei could see lights on in the diner on the other side of the street. Toby King's restaurant was open every day of the year, barring Thanksgiving and Christmas Day, he'd told her, and he wasn't kidding!

"Wow, Mom, look at all that snow!"

Lorelei glanced around and saw the remote on the coffee table. "Put the TV on, and I'm sure they will have snow totals on there."

Beth rushed to the table and switched on the flat panel. A news channel was on, and sure enough, they had people standing out in the cold, giving updates. Washington, DC had gotten eight inches of snow, and areas south and north had gotten way more. Fredericksburg was as close as she could see to where they were, and they'd had sixteen inches. It wasn't quite the storm of the decade, but it had come close.

"Did you ever see so much snow?" Beth asked.

Lorelei couldn't help smiling in return; the excitement of her ten-year-old was contagious. "When you were around four, there was a bigger storm, but you probably don't remember that," she replied.

"Can we go out in it later, Mom?"

Lorelei was about to say yes when she realized they would need to find their snow gear first. "Do you remember where we put your snow pants and boots?" She asked, hopefully. Beth's face fell, and she shook her head. "Don't worry, I know they're in one of the boxes from the car, and Earl left them downstairs in the stairwell, I'll find them soon enough!"

Beth grabbed her in a bear hug and danced her around the rental unit, and Lorelei was glad to see her daughter so happy. No matter how hard things might be at first, leaving Malcolm had been the smartest decision she'd made in a long time.

Waking up on the futon he'd donated to the office for the break room reminded Jefferson why he'd gotten rid of the thing. He had a crick in his neck and his back, and it served him right. He'd known his SUV needed servicing, and he'd still left it too long. He'd used one of Earl's trucks to clear the snow, and then he'd walked back to the diner after and found his car just wouldn't start.

Everyone else had gone home by that time. Even Toby called it a night just after two, so Jefferson decided to walk across the road to his office. It was preferable to the walk home since his driveway still needed plowing. He'd used his single cup coffee maker to make three cups of decaf to thaw out his extremities, and on the third one, he'd felt almost human again. There were emergency blankets and other supplies in the storage room, and he'd made himself a bed on the futon. He just hadn't remembered it being so uncomfortable.

He folded up the bedding and was on his way to the storage room when he saw her climbing the stairs. She was wearing a cute nightshirt that only made it as far as her thighs, a sweater over the top, and socks. His mouth went dry at the sight of her bare legs, and he figured he should make himself known to her. "Morning ma'am," he said, and she jumped so hard she dropped the box she was carrying.

"What are you doing here?" She asked, sounding defensive.

"My office is under Toby's apartments, he owns the whole building," Jefferson answered. He couldn't help noticing her hands were shaking, and not entirely from the cold, he guessed. "I'm sorry if I scared you."

She squared her shoulders at that, looking ready for a fight, and then she looked him up and down. He'd had women do that to him before, but this time it was far from an invitation. Time to mend a few fences, he decided. "Do you need help to carry those up?" He offered, nodding to the remaining boxes in the stairwell. There were three flights of steps for her to negotiate, and he could tell she was considering his offer.

"Yes, I could use some help," she admitted grudgingly. "Thank you."

"You're welcome," he allowed her to pick up the box she had dropped and picked up the other two. God, they were heavy as bricks, he thought. Then she started up the stairs again, and he realized how short that nightshirt was and how much she was about to reveal of those smooth, toned legs. Being the good guy that he was, he knew he had to get ahead of her on the stairs. He passed her on the first flight, then jogged to the top hallway and waited for her there.

She gave him a strange look but didn't say anything. He'd known many guys in college who would have been only too happy to follow her, enjoying the view. But thinking some pervert might do that to his sister made him more than a little uncomfortable.

Beth was standing in the doorway to the apartment, watching him suspiciously when Lorelei made it to the top. She couldn't help envying how easy the three flights of stairs had been for his long legs.

"Beth, can you take this box into the bedroom, I think your snow gear is in it?" she asked. The words worked like magic, her daughter's stern face melted into a beaming smile, and she grabbed the box out of Lorelei's arms and disappeared with it. "You can just leave those there," she said, but he raised his eyebrows skeptically. "You don't think I can move them in here myself?"

She didn't know why she'd felt challenged, but the smile spreading across his face was nothing short of miraculous. Oh, he had beautiful teeth and dimples when he smiled, and the lines fanning out beside his dark eyes said he laughed a lot, she thought. She felt an unexpected tug of attraction for him and then squashed that inappropriate thought.

He placed the boxes carefully on the floor and leaned back on the doorjamb and folded his arms. Excellent muscle definition and his legs in those blue jeans just went on forever. When she looked up and met his eyes, she knew he had caught her looking, and her cheeks burned. She reached for the bottom box to cover her embarrassment, fully intending to lift both at once. When she tried the first time, she could only get the boxes an inch above ground before her arms gave out. What the hell was in them? She wondered, and then remembered Beth had insisted on bringing all her books in the car.

He laughed humorlessly. Lorelei felt her dander rising, as her Grandma had called it whenever she dared to disagree with her, which wasn't often. She tried again with all her might this time and raised the boxes an inch or two, bending her knees so she wouldn't break her back. Her legs almost gave way, and her calves were burning from the effort of trying to take a step, but she refused to quit.

He stepped in front of her then, his smile gone, and took the boxes from her hands. His eyes seemed almost black, and he looked annoyed like he had when she wouldn't get in his car. When he was mad, he clenched his jaw, she realized. It emphasized his dimples, but she doubted he would appreciate the thought. She shifted her gaze and stared at his chest, refusing to meet his eyes, willing him to move.

He stepped away then and carried the boxes into the living room, put them on the coffee table, and then walked back to where she was still standing by the door. He worked his jaw back and forth as if he were trying to work off his irritation with her. She knew it would be churlish not to say thank you, but something about the man just made her act contrary to normal. Before she could even say anything, he walked out the door and started down the stairs again. Then he paused and turned and looked back up at her. "You are one of the most stubborn women I have ever met," he said in a slow, measured tone.

She wanted to say you just met me, you don't know me, but she knew she couldn't argue with him. She *had* refused to get in his car; she *had* just acted like an idiot pretending she could carry the boxes of books, and she knew that she had always been a little stubborn. It was another thing her grandmother had frequently pointed out when she was growing up. "I'm sorry, we've been going through a tough time lately, and I suppose I wanted to prove I don't need anyone's help," she said.

"You mean, *my* help," he corrected her tersely before he turned and jogged down the remaining stairs.

Ugh! She sighed after he was out of sight, admitting to herself he was right. She hated that he had her pegged so quickly, but nothing he'd seen so far would suggest she were anything but a royal pain in the butt. She walked over to the coffee table and hefted a box onto the floor.

"Whoa Mom, flashing much!" Beth walked out of the bedroom, laughing.

Lorelei glanced back and saw her legs almost up to her underwear, reflected in the glass doors of the wall cabinet. Thank goodness Jefferson had left already, she thought, and then her mouth dropped open, and she closed her eyes.

"Mom?"

Lorelei stood atop the coffee table and looked down at Beth. "Tell me you can't see up my nightshirt?"

Beth frowned. "Am I supposed to lie?"

Lorelei climbed down off the table, feeling her cheeks burning and excused herself to the bathroom. There was no way Jefferson Cooper hadn't gotten a fantastic view up her nightshirt as she was walking up the stairs earlier. Even though she didn't know him at all, it explained his Herculean sprint up the stairs with the boxes of books. Since he didn't sport a wedding band, she assumed he was single, and clearly, he was a gentleman. She knew if Malcolm had been behind a strange woman in the same situation, he would have soaked up every second. He would probably have gotten his cell phone out too.

Lorelei added, apologize to Jefferson, to her list again. Still, at least this time, he wasn't a total stranger, although somehow that made it harder. Lifting her nightshirt to her waist, she checked herself out in the mirror. She wasn't as toned as some women, and she hadn't been running in a long time, but she'd always thought her legs were her best feature, despite her lack of height. Had Jefferson liked what he saw? She wondered. Did she want him to have liked what he saw?

Oh God, it was as if she was in high school all over again, and she wanted the cute boy to find her pretty. Except in high school, she wasn't running away from a toxic marriage or stuck in some small town in a snowstorm waiting until she could sort out her car issue.

She was thirty-four years old, not fourteen, and yet her reaction to Jefferson Cooper was making her feel things she knew she had no right to be feeling at this point in her life, and it wasn't fair. And did the man have to be so freaking gorgeous? He looked like he'd just walked out of a GQ photo shoot or something, and the way his jeans fit was almost sinful.

Lorelei groaned at her reflection in the bathroom mirror. It had been quite a while since she and Malcolm last had sex. To be honest, it had never been a spectacular experience, but it explained her hormonal reaction to Jefferson! She'd only been with two men in her life. One had been her high school sweetheart from senior year, Joe, Beth's Dad. The other man was Malcolm Miller, and he'd only been in their lives for a year.

Joe Hannah had been the sweetest, kindest man and a good husband and father until an accident had robbed him of his life. Malcolm was a charmer when he needed to be, but when he didn't get what he wanted, he was anything but. What was Jefferson Cooper in comparison? She wondered. Dangerous, her mind supplied, which meant the apology could wait, staying out of his way was a far safer plan!

Jefferson tried to get the image of Lorelei's legs out of his mind, but he couldn't. No matter what he set his mind to in the office, those legs would just pop right back into his thoughts, every smooth, curvy inch of them. Since catching up on paperwork wasn't the distraction he'd been looking for, he decided to walk across to Toby's for a short stack and to see what was going on in town. Toby was like a one-man CNN for Lake Thomas and that, Jefferson thought, should take his mind off a particular stubborn stranger he kept encountering.

He shrugged into a down jacket and pulled on his work boots before stepping outside. Wow, it was still frigid out, he thought. The snow looked pretty enough, but he knew it would be a cruddy brown mess in a few days, and it would wreak havoc with local businesses, including his own.

A cloud of heat enveloped him as the door to Toby's swung open, and he went inside. He found himself face to face with Coop and his deputy Artie. They were carrying steaming travel coffee mugs, and Jefferson looked out of the window and saw the sheriff's SUV parked next to his own.

"Morning little brother," Coop said, smirking.

"Go ahead, say it," Jefferson told him. He knew his brother was dying to say I told you so about his car needing a service.

"No need," said Coop. "Earl put a new battery in for you this morning, the one in there was almost antique. He said you should either come by for an oil change or go shopping for a new car while you still have something to trade-in. You can settle up the bill for the battery with Dad later."

Jefferson grimaced. He'd had the Explorer for over ten years, and it had been a great vehicle, but it was showing its age, and the repair bills were adding up. "I don't have time to go car shopping," he grumbled.

"Well, don't call me when your alternator goes, and you need a ride," Coop said.

"Or your engine dies altogether," Artie chimed in.

Great, now the deputy was getting in on the act. Jefferson waved them off as they headed out the door and turned to find Toby waiting for him at the counter.

"Don't mind them," Toby said with a genial smile. "But if you go looking for another vehicle, I know some great places in Stafford. I can get you a good deal."

Jefferson smiled. Toby knew everyone, and if he didn't know someone personally, he knew someone who did. "Thanks, I may have to take you up on that."

"So, let me see what you'll order today, how about a short stack and some bacon on the side, with a steaming cup of coffee?"

As always, the man remembered his favorites, Jefferson thought, wondering how on earth he did it. He headed for a booth by the window to get a better view of the snow, and as he sat down, he saw them come around the side of his building. The little girl was wearing a full snowsuit, and the woman was wearing jeans and a puffy thigh-length coat. They both had snow boots, hats, and gloves on, stomping their way through the rolling drifts alongside Main Street.

Jefferson watched them struggle to make snowballs, but it was so cold outside the snow was in no mood to cooperate. He remembered similar snowstorms as a kid, and they were just no fun because the snow wouldn't stick together, which meant no fights, no snowmen to build, and no snow forts either. His sister Grace would not be happy with this!

"They're having fun out there," Toby commented as he brought the food.

Jefferson smiled and nodded. The little girl had a sadness in her eyes that said everything had not been perfect in her life, as did the Mom. It was nice to see them smiling and relaxed. He watched as Beth scooped up the sandy snow and shoved as much as she could down her mother's collar. Lorelei shuddered and laughed as she tried to stop it descending any further.

"I remember seeing you do that to young Gracie when you were a boy," Toby said wistfully.

He remembered too. Having a younger sister was always fun because you had to be so much more responsible once you were in high school. Still, if you had a little sister, well, you had to be silly for her sake, didn't you?

The phone rang then, and Toby hurried off. Jefferson continued to enjoy watching the snowball fight across the street while he ate his breakfast.

The snow was liberating! Lorelei thought. Beth was laughing and acting like a ten-year-old should for once, instead of worrying about things she was too young to be thinking about, namely her mother's husband. It was funny, but until recently, Lorelei hadn't noticed that Beth refused to call Malcolm her stepfather. She only ever referred to him as Malcolm, my mother's husband, which spoke volumes about how she felt about him, Lorelei supposed. Today though, Beth was acting like a kid, and it was beautiful to see.

"This snow is weird," Beth complained as she tried for the umpteenth time to form it into any kind of solid shape.

"I think it's too cold," Lorelei replied and saw her daughter's disbelieving look. "I'm serious!"

"How can it be too cold for snow?"

Lorelei laughed. "Because it is! Now we have ten more minutes, and then we'll go across the street for some hot chocolate and doughnuts."

Beth's eyes lit up at the suggestion. "Can we go there now? I'm kind of bored already, and I love doughnuts."

Lorelei wrapped her daughter in a bear hug and dragged her across the deserted street to the diner. They had eaten little this morning because they'd only had a few snacks left from the car, so doughnuts and hot chocolate were just what they needed.

She noticed him as soon as they opened the door. The diner was cozy with the roaring fireplace putting out some welcome heat. There were only a few other customers. Toby was behind the counter, and Jefferson was in the booth right by the front window. She wondered if he had been watching them, but she didn't turn his way because she didn't want him to know she'd noticed him and how crazy did that sound?

"Princesses, what can I get you on this snow-covered morn?" Toby asked cheerfully.

Beth giggled. "We would like two hot chocolates with whipped cream and marshmallows, please," she said primly.

"And two doughnuts too, please," Lorelei said, retrieving her wallet from her coat pocket.

The bell over the door dinged, and another Cooper brother came in and walked straight to the counter.

"Good morning," Jackson said and then looked over his shoulder and nodded at his brother.

Lorelei could easily see the family resemblance in daylight. Same bone structure, same coloring, and eyes but slightly different build and height. She caught Jefferson's gaze then and didn't quite know how to react, so she smiled awkwardly, and he smiled back in much the same way. Great, she thought, any inkling of doubt gone that she'd flashed him earlier. He looked as uncomfortable as she felt, well, that was just awesome!

"Coffee, scrambled eggs, bacon, and beans," Toby declared.

"You got it," Jackson replied and went over to the booth by the window to slide in opposite his brother.

Beth walked over to a booth closer to the fireplace and further away from the door, and they sat down with Lorelei facing toward the main entrance. Jackson acknowledged her from his table. She nodded in return, thanking her lucky stars his brother was pointing the other way.

Their hot chocolates came quickly. Beth had worked up a healthy appetite in the snow, finished her glazed doughnut in record time, and then ate half of her mother's. They made quick work of their drinks too and paid before heading for the door.

The two brothers were still sitting in their booth, so Lorelei had to acknowledge them out of politeness. She noticed she got a far warmer response from Jackson but dismissed the thought because she didn't know either of them well enough to make a fair judgment.

As they walked across the road, Beth chattered on, planning a day of movie watching. Lorelei just hoped when they returned to Toby's for dinner later that a certain Cooper brother would not be in residence.

Jackson was the king of reading body language, and Jefferson waited for the inevitable cross-examination. "What did you do now?"

Nice, Jefferson thought, there was no doubt in his brother's mind he'd done something. "I have no idea what you're talking about."

"*Really*?" Jackson continued, not easily dissuaded. "So, you barely looked at her, she looked embarrassed as hell, and you *still* claim there is no story there?"

Jefferson decided it was easier to give Jackson the abridged version, leaving out a few of the pertinent details, but his brother knew there was more.

"What did you do, argue about her not getting in your car last night?" Jackson asked.

Time to just rip that bandage off, Jefferson decided because Jackson wasn't going to give up. "I helped her carry boxes upstairs this morning."

"You said that already."

"Before that, she didn't see me as she was going up the stairs," He continued, trying to avoid having to say too much.

"And?" His brother was far too astute and pushy.

"Okay, she was on the stairs in a nightshirt thing and a sweater, I offered to carry boxes she had in the stairwell and when she started up the stairs again…" He didn't have to finish the sentence, and Jackson's expression said it all.

"Wow, fast work, brother."

"Hey, you know I'm not that kind of guy!" he protested.

His brother nodded. "True. So, how were her legs?"

Jefferson looked away but kicked out one of his long legs under the booth table and caught his brother in the shin. "Ow, jeez, that good, huh?"

"Enough already," Jefferson pleaded.

"She's pretty," Jackson said.

"So?"

"Nothing. Just wanted to see how you'd react to that," Jefferson's brother said, grinning in much the same way Coop had earlier.

"Say nothing to Grace or Dad," Jefferson cautioned.

Jackson reluctantly agreed he wouldn't. Jefferson wondered a little at his brother's quick agreement but decided he'd had enough ribbing for one morning.

He finished his coffee and left enough to cover both bills before saying his goodbyes and going out to his car. It started the first time thanks to the new battery, and he drove home and found his driveway plowed all the way to the garage. No doubt, one of his brothers had done it for him on seeing his car parked at Toby's. He grabbed a shovel off the porch and cleared the path to the house while trying not to think about Lorelei's legs. Or, how very much he'd wanted to slide his hand up her thigh to find out if her skin felt as velvety smooth as it looked.

THREE

I can't believe it, Lorelei thought, as she bustled about King Toby's six days after arriving in Lake Thomas. Toby had offered her a job because Joyce, one of his five regular waitresses, had slipped on refrozen snow and sprained her ankle. Lorelei had jumped at the chance on the condition Toby would allow her to pay towards rent on the apartment they were using. He'd reluctantly agreed but insisted she kept her tips, and she'd been working the breakfast shift for three days now.

Most of the customers were truck drivers and travelers who made a detour from the interstate because they'd been in before or read the Yelp reviews. Many locals came in too on their way to jobs in Fredericksburg and DC and other surrounding places. In the summer months, Toby told her he tripled his staff to deal with the lake home rental traffic and the campground visitors.

Lorelei hadn't realized how hard it was to be on her feet for several hours, but she loved the job more than she would ever have imagined. She'd quit her office job a few days before moving, but she hadn't enjoyed cubicle life anyway. She did love talking to the people of Lake Thomas, though, who made her realize the kind of place she was looking to settle down in. The best part of the job was that Toby let Beth camp out in the back room while she was working.

She felt no peace when she thought about Malcolm, though. He hadn't called or emailed since she'd been in Lake Thomas. Although she really didn't want to hear from him, she'd been expecting some reaction. She'd finally called his cell and discovered it had been disconnected. She was trying to work up the courage to go into Cooper Law and talk to Jefferson's brother about starting divorce proceedings. But if she went to see Jackson, she might have to encounter Jefferson, and she was still trying to avoid him. She knew she was a coward, but he made her feel like a desirable woman again, and that felt wrong when she was still a married woman.

Although Malcolm's silence was unnerving for her, it allowed Beth to adjust to life without him, which was a good thing. Lorelei knew her daughter was often nervous around men, even her best friend's father, which was all Malcolm's fault. It was like Ruby had been her guardian angel, Lorelei thought, and she'd sent her to the one place she could lick her wounds and rebuild her life.

She knew she had to stay long enough in Lake Thomas to scatter Ruby's ashes, but with the cold and snow, that could be a few weeks. Beth asked if they could stay in the area, and Lorelei called the elementary school to see if they had room for another student and found out they did.

"There's a customer that might be of use to you!" Toby said, pointing to a woman who'd just walked in.

Lorelei walked over with her notepad, sending Toby an amused look. He had a way of saying things without directly explaining himself, which was both charming and unique. After just a few days, she was getting used to his quirky ways. "What can I get for you?" Lorelei smiled at the customer occupying the booth closest to the roaring fire.

"Thermal underwear would be good for starters," the woman laughed. "I'm Grace Cooper. I think you've met at least two of my brothers?"

Lorelei shook the offered hand. "The Coopers? I think I've met three. Nice to meet you. I'm Lorelei Hannah."

"You called the school today, the secretary told me. Are you thinking of staying here for a while?" Grace asked, and Lorelei wondered if the woman ever stopped smiling, because her cheerfulness was infectious.

"We may stay until the end of the school year until I can get a few things sorted out. It seems like a nice town," Lorelei saw the woman's smile widen.

"We like it, but we might be a tiny bit biased. I've lived here my whole life, except for college," Grace said.

"How many brothers do you have?"

"Just the three you mentioned, which is more than enough, I'm sure you'd agree. Makes dating anyone a total nightmare, especially when one carries a weapon routinely!" Grace laughed, but Lorelei could tell how much she loved her siblings.

"You must take after your Mom," she said. Grace had fiery red hair that hung halfway down her back, and she was only a few inches taller than Lorelei herself was.

Grace shrugged. "I may never know the answer to that question. I'm adopted."

"Oh, I'm sorry, I didn't...," Lorelei stammered, at a loss for how she could appropriately apologize for her colossal gaffe.

"It's okay," Grace laughed. "Someone abandoned me as a baby in the back seat of my Dad's car, wrapped only in a baby blanket. My Dad was a deputy at the time, and my parents adopted me, eventually. The rest, as they say, is history."

Lorelei admired Grace's unwavering spirit. "I'm sorry, I don't think I ever took your order. What would you like?"

Jefferson's sister ordered a hot chocolate and some of Toby's homemade cookies. Lorelei slipped out back to check on Beth, who had her head buried in a drawing book. "You okay out here?"

"Yeah, do you like my dragon?" Beth asked, holding up her sketchbook.

Lorelei stared at the drawing in surprise. She might be Beth's Mom, but she could tell the picture was better than the average child her age could do. "That is an awesome dragon. You have some serious talent, young lady, and I'm not just saying that!"

Beth beamed and then buried her face in her drawing again, and Lorelei hurried back to get Grace's order to her booth. Grace took the steaming mug from her and warmed her hands before taking a long sip. "I so need one of those machines to make these at home, but then I'd put on about ten pounds a week in winter because I'd be drinking this stuff morning, noon and night!" She joked.

"Beth is partial to it too, she already had one this morning," Lorelei said.

"Is she here? Maybe I can meet her, I don't teach fourth grade, I specialize in art, but Mrs. Evanston does, and she's fantastic," Grace explained.

"Beth would love to meet her art teacher!"

Lorelei asked Toby if she could take her coffee break a little early, then took Grace through to the backroom to introduce her to Beth.

He didn't want to go across to get lunch, Jefferson thought irritably, and all because of a particular curvy newcomer to town. The only problem was that the main grocery store they shopped at was about five miles away, and they didn't have time to go with their heavy workload.

Their newest client, The Mary Douglas Center, was an exclusive spa being built on the far side of their small town. It would cater to high-end clientele and even have a rehab facility if approved by the town council. They were handling a lot of real estate deals for the locals of Lake Thomas, who were eager to sell small portions of their properties surrounding the spa. Who could blame them for wanting a little extra cash in this flagging economy, especially from land that was rocky and hilly and hard to use?

Jackson suggested working through lunch. Jefferson drew rock to paper and lost, so here he was, unable to avoid Lorelei anymore because she was working in King Toby's now. How the hell had that happened so fast, anyway? He wondered.

As he waited at the counter for his order, he heard voices coming from the backroom, all of them female and one he recognized well. He knew Grace had an unexpected day off because of the school's heating system breaking down. His sister was laughing, which was something she often did. Then, he heard her talking about Gloria Evanston, who'd been at Lake Thomas Elementary so long she'd been *his* fourth-grade teacher.

Lorelei was planning to stay in town for a while, he thought, and how exactly was that meant to make him feel? His mind flashed back to those surprisingly sexy legs he'd glimpsed. He couldn't explain why, but he was sure her impromptu peep show hadn't been intentional. It didn't mean he hadn't been entertaining a few steamy fantasies about that encounter, though.

He heard Grace ask Lorelei why she hadn't gotten into his car before the snowstorm had hit. He knew it was wrong to eavesdrop on them, but he wouldn't get a straight answer if he asked himself, so he waited, wondering what her answer would be.

"He's kind of scary," Beth answered first.

"Jeff? Scary?" Grace snorted out a laugh. "He's a little serious, maybe, but I've never thought of him as scary before."

"He's just so tall and, um, imposing," Lorelei said. "He wasn't in the best mood, either. He said he had a headache."

"Ah, you got grumpy, Jefferson, poor you!" Grace said.

He couldn't argue with that; he had been tired and cranky, and he'd never thought about how his height might make him seem threatening to someone as petite as Lorelei. Most teens were taller than her, he thought, but they sure weren't built like her.

"He's a good guy though and a hard worker," Grace continued. "He's someone I always want in my corner, even if he isn't the most spontaneous or patient person you're ever likely to meet. He's the planner in our family. The one who makes sure we all know where we're supposed to be. If it weren't for my brother, I swear, I'd never have made it through college and become a teacher."

Great, he thought, I'm dependable. I'm every woman's dream man, he thought cynically. He wasn't sure why it annoyed him so much, but it did. His sister didn't have a mean bone in her body, and she had meant no offense by what she'd said. She'd bruised his ego, he realized, but that served him right for eavesdropping at all. Nice, dependable guys always seemed to finish last in this world. His experience with his ex, Stephanie, attested to that.

Toby finished the sandwiches and handed the order over on a cardboard tray. Jefferson paid him before walking back across the street to his office. Jackson shot him a quizzical look as he walked in. "What put a crank in your pants?"

Jefferson ignored him and handed out the sandwiches and drinks.

"Okay then," His twin knew when to leave something well enough alone. He wasn't even entirely sure why he was so mad, or maybe, he wasn't ready to admit why it mattered so much what Lorelei thought of him, it just did.

Lorelei had finished her shift for the day and was watching the news while Beth did math and science work on her tablet. They were talking about more snow on the nightly news, and Lorelei knew Beth would be mad about it this time as she wanted to start her new school on Monday. Luckily, Lorelei had gotten all Beth's transcripts from her old school before leaving Alexandria, so there was nothing to delay them, except Mother Nature.

It was nice to be able to sit and relax, she thought, not stressing out because Malcolm would be home soon and not wondering what his mood would be. After a day of working in a small cafe in a job she was sorely underqualified for, she got to watch some TV. One of the reasons she liked the town so much was because everyone was so friendly. Lake Thomas had a real sense of community. Toby said they had their fair share of curmudgeons too, but the picture he and Grace painted made her want to stay in the town, at least until the end of the school year.

She looked down at her fingernails and grimaced. Waitressing had wrecked her manicure because she couldn't seem to hold more than one plate in her hands at a time. Working on her nails looked like a great way to pass the time until Beth was ready for some dinner. If only she could find her purse. Lorelei closed her eyes, whispered a mild curse word, and stood up.

"Hey, Beth," she said, standing in the doorway to her daughter's room.

Beth removed her headphones and paused the science tutorial engrossing her. "This is so much fun, Mom, it's all about building a robot. Can we do that sometime?"

Lorelei shrugged. "Sure, we can add it to our list of summer vacation activities, but first, I need to go across the street because I left my purse at King Toby's. Will you be okay here for a few minutes by yourself?"

Beth rolled her eyes dramatically, a look she had been perfecting lately.

"Okay, I know you're ten, and it's only for five minutes, but if there is an emergency, what would you do?" Lorelei quizzed.

"Call 911, call out for help, leave the building if it's on fire, go downstairs to the parking lot. Mom, I got this, you take longer than that in the shower, and I survive. I will be fine!" Beth sounded cross, and Lorelei held her hands up in mock surrender.

Beth was right. She did take longer in the shower, she realized, as she jogged across the street, pulling her cardigan tightly around herself to fend off the chill. The door to Toby's dinged as she went in, and he looked up from his newspaper and frowned at her.

"Woman, do you not have the sense you were born with? It's freezing out there!" he scolded her.

Lorelei laughed. "Must be my day for forgetting things, I left my purse here earlier, now I forget my coat, what next?" She quickly grabbed her bag and gave Toby and his sports section a quick wave before rushing back into the cold air and crossing over to the other side of the street. She almost ran into Jackson Cooper as he came out of the law offices situated under her apartment.

"Are you going around the back to get into your place?" he asked with a smile.

Lorelei couldn't help thinking how much like Jefferson he was, even though they were non-identical twins. Yet Jackson made her feel nothing at all, whereas the mere thought of his brother could launch a flock of giant butterflies in her stomach.

"I am going in," she said.

"Then be my guest and cut through the office since you're crazy enough to be out here without a coat on. Our exit is through the kitchen at the back," he offered cheerfully.

Lorelei hesitated for a split second, but Jackson noticed.

"He's not there. He went home to change his shirt. He dumped a whole mug of coffee on himself. White shirts and black coffee sure don't mix well!" He smiled kindly.

Lorelei didn't want to delve into how Jackson knew she was hesitating because of Jefferson. Clearly, she wasn't great at hiding her emotions because even Beth picked up on her moods like they were on radar sometimes.

"Thanks, Jackson," Lorelei said as she walked over to the unlocked door and stepped into the warm office. She watched him run across to Toby's and mused at how everyone in the town just loved the diner. Then, she took a good look around the Cooper brothers' law offices because she couldn't resist.

Whoever had decorated the place had done a fantastic job, she had to admit. Everything was very sleek and minimalist, but it was still welcoming. Expensive Law books lined the walls in the waiting area. There was a giant L-shaped leather couch against the wall and a table with a variety of magazines. There was even a wooden box in the corner with a few kids' books and toys, which Lorelei thought was a nice touch for clients who had to bring their kids with them.

There were two enormous oak desks and then a room to one side with the door shut. It was probably a conference room or private office, Lorelei mused. It was clear the brothers worked side by side at their desks in the main office. There was a door at the end with an illuminated EXIT sign above it, so she headed that way.

She knew it had to lead to the back of the building because the stairs she used to access the upstairs apartment were right outside the law firm's rear door. Cutting through the building was probably the smartest thing she had done today, she decided.

She froze as she opened the door. As she had expected, it led to the kitchen. Jefferson was on the far side of that room with his back to her. He was already shirtless, and she watched as he stripped off a white undershirt too and tossed it by the sink. Dear God, there wasn't a single ounce of fat on the man, she thought, watching the tanned muscles of his back ripple when he tore open a dry cleaner's bag and took out a clean shirt. Apparently, he hadn't needed to go home, despite Jackson's assumption.

I should say something, she thought, but her breath had lodged somewhere in her diaphragm, and she was sure the only noise she would be capable of was a strangled squeak. Her hand was still on the doorknob, for fear releasing it would alert Jefferson to her presence. It was lust she was feeling, she decided, brought on by abstinence, and nothing more.

She watched from behind as he began buttoning his shirt, then he turned and saw her. She stayed frozen in the doorway, willing her brain to come up with something inane to say before she could make a dash for freedom.

"Jackson offered me a shortcut," she said in a breathy voice, mustering the semblance of a smile as she took a step towards the exit via the far side of the kitchen. Jefferson stepped in front of her at the last minute, forcing her to pause by the double sink. He hadn't fully buttoned his shirt, and she could see an enticing column of lightly tanned skin, and then a hint of some dark chest hairs.

"Look at me, Lorelei," He said in a low voice. She couldn't help herself; she looked up into his smoky charcoal eyes. He looked back into hers, and then his gaze dropped to her mouth. He was thinking about kissing her, she realized. She knew she should step away or do something, but she couldn't make her feet work.

"Tell me you don't want this," he said, but she just watched, mesmerized, as he lowered his mouth towards hers and put his hands on her waist. "Lorelei?" His eyes flicked quickly from her mouth to her eyes again, and she knew he'd seen the same yearning there.

The kiss started out slowly, gently probing, and it felt so good, she thought guiltily. Jefferson's lips traveled leisurely across her cheek and down the soft skin of her neck. She felt her knees give way at the incredible sensations he was evoking. He didn't let her fall. He caught her, lifting her, so she was sitting on the edge of the counter by the sink. She longed to wrap her legs around his waist and drag him closer still, but she didn't dare.

She did let him slide his warm hands under her cardigan, and those strong hands found their way beyond the tee shirt she was wearing and made their way slowly up her back. Any second now, he would find out she'd taken off her bra when she'd gotten home because the straps were digging into her shoulders, she thought. Still, she didn't care because all she wanted was to feel this man's hands on her body.

The minute Jefferson turned around and saw Lorelei watching him putting on his shirt, he'd known this would happen. He'd wanted to touch her for days. He'd wanted to slide his hands up those shapely legs to find out if they were as silky as they looked. He'd wanted *her* period.

When he'd lifted her onto the kitchen counter, he'd expected her to object, to push him away and stop him. He'd half expected a slap for that first tentative kiss, and when it hadn't happened, he'd kissed her neck, and she'd made a sexy little noise in the back of her throat as her legs buckled slightly. That was the point he'd realized she needed this as much as he did.

She was a lot taller sitting on the countertop, and the skin of her back felt so smooth under her tee-shirt. He moved his mouth to hers again and brushed her lips softly with his own. Her eyes were closed, he noticed, as he stepped back slightly, and her chest was rising and falling rapidly. He slid his hands further up her back and felt her arch towards him. Then his rational brain stopped working. For the love of God, she wasn't wearing a stitch under that shirt, he thought raggedly.

He backed up and looked down at her parted cardigan. The pebble-hard peaks of her very feminine curves stood out against the cotton tee. His mouth went dry at the same moment that areas south went hard. He stared into her eyes as he slid his hands oh so slowly around to cup those curves and watched as the blue of her eyes deepened several shades and her lids drooped. "Tell me to stop, and I will," he breathed. *Don't tell me to stop,* he prayed. Lorelei looked him right in the eyes and slid her hands up to cover his and then helped continue their journey to those yearning peaks.

What are you doing? Lorelei's rational brain screamed inside her head as she moved his hands to where she wanted to feel them. She was making out with a man who was virtually a stranger. Hell, this was way more than making out, she acknowledged. His hands were touching her intimately. His thumbs were rubbing back and forth across her nipples, causing an agony of sensation, and she wanted more, so much more. He stopped rubbing her breasts. She felt bereft until his arms slid around her waist and under her butt, lifting her into his arms while his mouth plundered mercilessly.

Then she heard a vaguely familiar sound. It nagged at the part of her brain that was still capable of functioning. What was it? She wondered, knowing she'd heard it before. She had her arms curled around his neck; her body pressed intimately to his. Suddenly, she remembered what the sound was, but what did the bell matter, anyway?

Crap! It was as if someone had thrown a bucket of icy water on her. The bell was on the door into Cooper Law, and she knew that because Toby's diner had one just like it. The doorbell meant someone was in the building and could well be heading this way. She pushed back from Jefferson, missing the touch of his lips instantly, and slid down his body until her feet hit the tiled floor. He looked flushed and puzzled. She could tell exactly when he heard footsteps coming, and then he was tugging her arm and pulling her out into the stairwell where the chilly air hit them hard.

"I have to go, Beth is alone upstairs," Lorelei stammered as she ran to the stairs and made a quick getaway. She heard him open the exterior door and go outside even though he still hadn't buttoned up his shirt. He would be freezing, she knew. But, the frigid air would be like a cold shower for a certain area of his anatomy she'd noticed as she'd slid over his body to the ground.

"Hi, Mom," Beth called to her as she walked into the apartment. "That was over five minutes, you know, thanks for trusting me!"

Lorelei mustered a smile and headed for her bedroom. Once inside, she closed the door and saw her flushed cheeks in the dressing-table mirror. There was other damning evidence of her arousal too. She grabbed her discarded bra and tore off her cardigan and tee-shirt, so she could put it back on. The soft cotton cups rubbed agonizingly against her sensitized breasts. What did you just do? She demanded of her reflection. She didn't know who she was anymore. She was behaving like a sex-starved teenager.

She had no answers, she realized as she donned the rest of her clothes. She was the new Lorelei Hannah, just like she'd promised she would be before she'd left Alexandria. It was like she was recreating herself from scratch, and apparently, the new Lorelei was as horny as hell!

FOUR

She couldn't avoid him forever, Lorelei finally admitted to herself on Monday as she got Beth ready for her first day at her new school. Jefferson had been working right below them all weekend with his brother. But, whenever she left the apartment to run an errand or go over to Toby's diner or just for some fresh air, she'd made sure he wasn't around. You're such a chicken, she thought and groaned.

"Mom?" Beth looked puzzled.

"I'm not going insane Beth, I have a few things on my mind," Lorelei reassured her.

"Is there something wrong?"

Lorelei smiled. Wrong? Her mind said yes, there was something wrong, she thought, but it had felt pretty darn right to her at the time. "I've just been avoiding someone, that's all."

"Malcolm?" Beth asked quietly.

"Him too!" Lorelei laughed, wondering when she'd become such a wuss. "I need to speak to the insurance company today, and I don't think they will have good news about our car, that's all." It was only a little white lie, she told herself because she did have a meeting in Fredericksburg with the insurance company while Beth was in school.

"Will you have to speak to Malcolm?" Beth was anxiously chewing on her fingernails as she asked.

"I can't call him, Beth, his cell number isn't working, I tried to call it already. Anyway, I will start the paperwork this week, so we can be free of him for good, I promise you," Lorelei said and gave her daughter a reassuring hug. "Now, do you have everything in your backpack? Your inhaler, lunch, pencil box, and notebooks?"

Lorelei watched as thoughts of school transformed her daughter from a worried child into an excited one. Beth loved school, and she couldn't wait to get settled into a new routine either. "Okay then, let's go wait outside for Grace to pick us up!"

Jefferson couldn't believe he'd let his sister talk him into giving Lorelei and Beth a ride to the elementary school. Grace had forgotten there was an early staff meeting and hadn't been able to get in contact with Lorelei to tell her.

Which was why he was sitting on the bench in front of the building, waiting to deliver the good news.

He was sure Lorelei had been avoiding him for the past two days. He'd heard her apartment door close abruptly too many times as he'd been coming in and out. He probably should apologize to her for that kiss, he thought, but in all honesty, there was no way in hell he felt sorry about what had happened. She had filled his dreams all weekend long. He kept replaying the R-rated scene in the kitchen, imagining where it might have gone if his brother hadn't returned. Just thinking about how soft her skin felt under his hands was pure torture.

He heard voices approaching, and his brain reluctantly squashed the replay running through his mind. "Hi," he managed a lame greeting as they looked at him in confusion. "Grace forgot she had a staff meeting this morning, and she couldn't get you on the phone. She asked me to give you a ride if that's okay with both of you?"

He said *both,* but his eyes were locked on Lorelei.

"I'm sorry, I forgot I switched the phone off last night. Anyway, the elementary school is not far, we can walk. Grace said, you're really slammed with work now, so you must be too busy to taxi us around," Lorelei heard the words tumbling out of her mouth and saw Beth frown.

"It's about a mile from here to the school, that's quite a walk, and it's chilly this morning," Jefferson kept his tone reasonable to avoid coming across as a jerk again.

"Mom, can we take the ride, please? I don't want to wheeze on my first day, it would be so totally embarrassing," Beth pleaded.

He watched Lorelei's expression soften into a smile as she looked down at her daughter. "If Mr. Cooper has the time to take us, we'll accept his offer of a ride." She looked at him then, and he smiled in relief. The Mr. Cooper crack was a little hard to swallow, but if Lorelei and Beth opted to walk rather than ride with him for a second time, Grace would never let him forget it.

"Oh no, I don't have my booster seat!" Beth panicked as they got to the parking lot. "Mom says I'm still too short to ride without one."

"Don't worry, I have one in my car already, Grace dropped it off this morning on her way to work. She figured yours needed replacing after the accident anyway," Jefferson said, taking Beth's backpack and opening the rear door for her to climb in.

Lorelei climbed in the back too to help Beth buckle up. She looked back at him as he stood holding the door, and she took a shaky breath in. "I think I'll sit back here with you, Beth, if that's okay with you, Mr. Cooper?"

He raised an eyebrow at her continued formality. "*Mr. Cooper* is my Dad. I think we know each other a little better than that, don't you?"

"Jefferson then," Lorelei amended in a low voice, holding his gaze for the briefest second.

A little eye contact was better than nothing, he conceded as he climbed into the driver's seat.

Everyone at the Lake Thomas Elementary School was so nice, Lorelei thought. She had a cramp in her hand as she finished up the last of the paperwork and handed it to the admissions clerk, Miss. Gilbert. The woman was also the school secretary and occasionally a substitute teacher because the school was small.

She walked with Beth to her new classroom, where her teacher, Mrs. Evanston, welcomed her new student warmly. "Have a good day, Beth," she said, as she walked away, forcing herself not to look back because Beth had already entered the classroom without even a backward glance.

The school nurse knew about Beth's asthma, and there was nothing left for Lorelei to do but walk out of the building. She took a deep breath, trying to keep her anxiety at bay. It was like the first day of kindergarten again, she thought as she called into the office on her way out.

"Your daughter will love it here, Mrs. Hannah," Miss. Gilbert told her kindly as Lorelei headed for the main entrance. "You have nothing to worry about." Lorelei nodded, but she knew she was only pretending for the sake of the admissions clerk.

She was halfway down the front walkway when she saw Jefferson's Explorer parked in the carpool lane. He got out and walked around to the passenger door. "Do you need a ride?"

"You haven't been here the whole time, have you?" She asked.

"No, just the last five minutes. I had a few errands to run, and Grace texted me to say you'd be ready to leave soon," he explained.

"I'm sorry Grace coerced you into this, but I will gladly take the ride, thank you. I have to be in Fredericksburg at ten o'clock," Lorelei reached for the door handle at the same moment he did but pulled back her hand quickly.

"I don't bite, Lorelei," he muttered as he opened the door for her and then walked around to the driver's side. She could feel the tension humming between them as they drove out of the parking lot.

"We need to clear the air," he announced.

"We really don't," Lorelei responded and heard him let out a frustrated breath.

"Okay, then we're making a detour," he said, turning abruptly down a small side road, which she realized was a driveway.

"What? I don't have time for a detour!" Lorelei complained.

"Tough!"

This was a lesson in how *not* to handle a delicate situation, Jefferson thought as he pulled up outside his house. Snow lay in frozen piles by the stone front steps, but the porch had been cleared, and the bench his grandfather had built for him was dry. "I will go sit over there and wait for you to come to talk to me, and I'm taking the keys," he said.

Lorelei stared out of the passenger window with her arms folded defensively. "Maybe I'll just slide on over as soon as you get out and hotwire your car and take off."

"Sure, you try that Lorelei, and I'll go wait over there until you give up on that idea," he was smiling as he said the words, hoping to defuse the situation. Then he saw her shoulders slump and start to shake. Shit, he thought, making her cry had not been part of his plan. What the hell was he supposed to do now?

It was the snort that gave her away. She wasn't crying at all, Jefferson realized she was laughing. That had to be a positive sign, right? He reached over and touched her cheek, meaning just to turn her face toward him, but he felt the spark of attraction flare again, and he was sure she felt it too. How long had it been since a woman had attracted him who intrigued him half as much as Lorelei? When she turned those cornflower blue eyes his way, still laughing, it was like Coop or Jack had sucker-punched him in the gut.

"Why are you looking at me like that?" Her smile faltered, and he didn't know how to answer her. *You're the most beautiful woman I've ever seen,* seemed trite and borderline sleazy. *You have an incredible smile,* was something you'd hear on one of those horrible reality dating shows. *You take my breath away,* he thought. He couldn't say that to her, he knew, but it was the truth. And she was still staring at him, he thought, waiting for an answer he couldn't give.

"So, what's happening in Fredericksburg?" He pulled the question out of the air, remembering she'd mentioned a meeting there earlier.

She took in a nervous breath. "I have to meet with the insurance company for the car." Then she sighed. "You're not really going to make me sit on that bench, so we can talk about the thing that happened in the kitchen, are you?"

He dropped his head. "No, I'm not, but I don't want you to hide out in your apartment because you don't want to face me either. I won't say I'm sorry about the kiss, because I'd be lying if I did, but if you are, we can just forget it ever happened." What was that joke about lawyer being code for *liar*? He could almost believe he meant what he was saying. Almost. If he were telling the truth, though, he wouldn't be holding his breath, waiting for her response.

She said nothing, so he buckled his seatbelt again and started the car. He was halfway through the U-turn on his driveway when he heard her voice. "I'm not sorry it happened either," she mumbled. "But it can't happen again, I just can't get involved with anyone right now, my life is a mess."

She watched him work his jaw back and forth out of the corner of her eye. She was sure he'd been hoping for a different answer. But, Lorelei knew she couldn't allow herself to get involved with anyone when she was still a married woman. It didn't matter that Malcolm had been a lousy husband. It didn't matter that he'd taken his fists to her one time and sent her to the emergency room. None of that mattered because, in her eyes, she was still a married woman.

Jefferson pulled into the parking lot behind his office. He hadn't spoken a word since she'd made her proclamation, and she couldn't blame him. She hadn't kissed him in the kitchen like a woman who didn't want to get involved with anyone. She'd kissed him as if her next breath depended on it and, God help her, just looking at his clenched jaw made her want to do it all over again.

Jefferson got out and walked to the passenger side and opened the door for her. She unbuckled her seatbelt and slid out of the car to the pavement, stumbling slightly, but he didn't reach out to steady her. He stared at her like she was a particularly taxing puzzle and one he didn't have a solution to. She knew he was waiting for her to move out of the way of the door, but she couldn't do it. He'd made her laugh so hard when she'd made that stupid comment about stealing his car, and now she wanted to cry like a baby.

"How are you getting to Fredericksburg? Do you need to borrow my car?" He floored her with the prosaic question.

"You'd lend me your car after everything I just said?" She couldn't believe it when he held out the keys without hesitation. "Did you see what I did to the last car I drove?"

He smiled, which she had to admit had been her goal. A little levity could go a long way in a stressful situation, she knew. "Thanks for the offer, but Toby is lending me his Ranger. You're a kind man, Jefferson Cooper."

He clenched his jaw hard and looked away, but not before she caught the look of distaste on his face. When he turned back, he had a bleak look in his eyes. "I'm not always a good guy, you know. I have a selfish streak a mile wide, just ask my family."

"I don't believe that for a minute," Lorelei whispered.

"Believe it!" He growled, and before she could catch her breath, his hands snaked around her waist, and he brought his face level with her own. His eyes were the deepest gray she'd ever seen them, and he was angry. Not angry in the way Malcolm got, she realized, this was different. "I'm going to kiss you, Lorelei, and I don't care if you don't want me to. I don't care if you don't want to be involved with me. I don't care what you want, period."

She was sure he intended his words to give her pause, but they had the opposite effect. She held her breath and stared up into his eyes, amazed because she'd never noticed before how long and black his eyelashes were, and she waited. He didn't follow through on what he'd said, and she could almost see the war going on inside his head. He was trying to act like a jerk, she realized, but he couldn't go through with it. He dropped his hands from her waist, and she missed their warmth at once.

She wanted to walk away. She should have walked away. She even managed to take a few steps, but then she turned back to see Jefferson drag a shaky hand through his unruly black hair. She knew she shouldn't, it was such a bad idea, but she reached up impulsively and grabbed his perfectly tied Windsor knot and pulled his head down to her level.

She wrapped her arms around his neck before she could change her mind, and planted an open-mouthed, impatient kiss on his lips. He reacted instantly, lifting her off her feet and pushing her up against his car. She felt his tongue glide against her teeth and slid her own out to meet it. He responded by crushing her in his arms so tightly she could barely breathe, but it felt amazing.

They came up for air eventually and just stared at each other. "I'm sorry," Lorelei stuttered. "I shouldn't have done that. I'm saying one thing, and I'm doing the complete opposite, and I don't think I know what the hell is going on in my head anymore."

"Do you want to rip all of my clothes off and kiss every inch of my body?" He asked. "Because that's what's going on in my head right now."

Lorelei's eyes widened, and she covered her burning cheeks with her hands. She felt like her entire body was blushing, but she couldn't utter a single word. They stared at each other for what felt like an eternity, then he finally stepped away, drawing in a ragged breath.

"You have an appointment in half an hour, and I need to get back to work," his voice was a masculine growl of frustration. "I don't know how I can walk into my office and think about anything but you, *but* I will walk away right now and do that." His voice was as steady as a rock, but she could see his hands were shaking as she watched him unlock the rear door into the building.

The door closed behind him, and she stared at it for the longest time. Eventually, she turned and headed around the building to Toby's. Jefferson had gotten under her skin so far, and so fast, it was mind-blowing. When he'd said he wanted to put his hands and mouth all over her naked body, she'd briefly entertained the idea of dragging him upstairs. Then her rational mind took over again. What am I going to do about him? She wondered.

Fix the things you can, Ruby had always said, leave the others for another day. She looked up at the gray winter sky. I'm taking your advice today, Ruby, she thought, and then she crossed the road and walked into the diner.

"I need to get my dry cleaning," Jackson announced as Jefferson walked in through the kitchen.

The California trip, Jefferson thought, he'd totally forgotten Jackson was flying out to the left coast in two days to meet with the owners of the retreat and finalize some paperwork.

"How was Beth on her first day?"

Jefferson smiled. "She seemed fine, more than fine, she was raring to go. I'm not so sure her Mom was as keen," he responded and watched as his brother smirked. "What?"

"Nothing brother, you seem to know our latest resident a lot better than most of us," Jackson tried to look innocent, but Jefferson wasn't buying it.

"I might go look at some car places while you're gone," he announced, attempting to steer the conversation away from Lorelei.

Jackson laughed hard at that. "Nice segue way!"

"Go get your dry cleaning, you idiot," he ordered, only half-joking. He wasn't ready to talk to anyone about Lorelei yet, because this was all too new to him.

As soon as Jackson left, he allowed himself to relive that last kiss from her, then immersed himself in contracts. Tedious paperwork sucked the sexy right out of you, he realized as he forced his mind onto something else. He needed time to figure out what was going on with Lorelei because he couldn't think straight whenever he was near her. He'd never felt that way about any woman before.

She was undoubtedly beautiful, but she was not his usual type. He'd never been involved with a woman who had a child before either. His most serious relationship had almost ended in marriage, but Stephanie had never been the maternal type. He'd hoped he could talk her into wanting kids after the wedding, and that should have been a red flag right there, he was finally able to admit.

Lorelei was about as far removed from Stephanie as possible. Physically, they were nothing alike. Lorelei was petite and curvy, where Stephanie was tall and athletic. Their coloring was different, too, and everything with Lorelei seemed spontaneous. Stephanie Gilbert had been more of a planner than Jefferson was himself. She had scheduled everything down to the last detail.

All of their vacations had been carefully arranged to showcase a specific image his fiancée insisted on cultivating to show what a great power couple they were. They'd attended all the right parties and socialized with all the right people. They'd built their client lists for *Dexter, Dillon, and Shaw,* climbing the corporate ladder towards partnerships. Until the whole thing had come crashing down around his ears, leaving him humiliated and betrayed in the worst way.

Was it really seven years ago that he'd met Stephanie? Jefferson thought. They'd met at work, and he'd fallen hard for her, and finally, after four years of dating, she'd agreed to marry him. He'd often wondered if his emotional state after his mother's death from cancer hadn't clouded his emotions to where he'd simply needed someone to anchor him. He'd imagined Stephanie to be that person, but he'd been wrong.

He hadn't known about her affair at all. He still couldn't believe he'd been *that* guy. The gullible boyfriend, accepting all her lies about her unexplained absences. If he hadn't forgotten his car keys one night, only a week before their wedding, he would never have seen the lights on in his boss's office. Nor would he have heard the crash that sent him running to investigate.

It hadn't been an intruder, far from it. He'd lost count of the number of times he'd relived that moment. He'd opened the door to find his naked fiancée sprawled across the senior partner's desk, being thoroughly serviced by his equally naked boss, Lance Dexter. They hadn't even noticed him for several seconds because they were too busy *noticing* the hell out of each other. He remembered his boss yelling at him and his fiancée, smiling like the Cheshire Cat from Alice in Wonderland. He'd walked out of the building that night and hadn't even gone back for his things. It had been a dark day in his life and the start of months of wallowing in his own misery.

When his brother had suggested they open a practice together in their hometown, he'd jumped at the chance. Who better to work with than Jackson?

Jefferson smiled as he worked steadily through a stack of paperwork he'd been putting off for days. Lance Dexter had done him a favor in retrospect, he admitted. His relationship with Stephanie had been doomed from the outset, but he hadn't wanted to see the truth. She'd wanted to be a partner at the law firm they worked at more than she would ever have wanted to be his partner in life. It was the epiphany he'd been waiting years for. Without Lorelei crashing headlong into his life, he wondered how much longer it would have taken him to realize.

If he needed any more proof that he'd gotten off lightly, it was his family's reaction to Stephanie. They'd tried so hard to like her and make her feel part of the family. They'd gone along with so many things she wanted to do. Jefferson knew it had been for him, but in the long run, she'd made it impossible for anyone to get close to her. She simply hadn't wanted to be part of his family because it didn't fit in with her long-term plans.

The door opened, and Jackson walked in, carrying several plastic garment bags. "Why are you smiling, big brother?" he asked.

Jefferson was only older by two minutes, but that had been enough when they were kids to spark many a fight. "No reason," he said, feeling more content than he had in years and all because of a certain petite blond.

FIVE

"You closed your account almost two weeks ago, Mrs. Hannah."

Lorelei stood at the counter in the bank in complete shock. She'd gone to her appointment with the insurance company. They'd given her a check for over five thousand dollars for her totaled car, which she knew was more than fair market value for a twelve-year-old PT Cruiser. Then she'd signed the vehicle over to them and used her GPS to find a branch of her bank nearby so that she could deposit the check. That was when the bottom had figuratively fallen out of her world.

Her accounts had been closed the day she'd moved out of her apartment, the cashier told her, all of them. She didn't have a checking account anymore or a savings account, and Beth's account was closed too. The cashier had called over the bank manager, and he wanted to contact the fraud department immediately. But, Lorelei was too shell-shocked to respond and simply walked out of the bank and back to Toby's truck.

She sat in the truck, staring blankly down the street. She was sure it wasn't a coincidence that the accounts had been closed on the day she'd moved out. Malcolm was friendly with some of the guys in their building. He had watched sports and shared a few beers with them, and it was likely one of them had told him she was packing up. He had to have been the one who closed the accounts, or he'd gotten someone to do it for him. It made no sense, though, because the bank said she had done it herself, with ID and everything, and she knew that wasn't right.

If she hadn't hit the deer, she might have noticed the bank issue earlier. But she'd taken cash out the day before the move, and thanks to Toby's generosity, she'd been able to leave her bank funds untouched, or so she'd thought.

Her head was pounding. That was when she accepted, she couldn't handle this all by herself. She needed help, and she only knew one person in law enforcement, Beth's friend's father and her friend, Detective Daniel Sullivan.

She called his cellphone, grateful that he picked up immediately. "Hi, Daniel, it's Lorelei," she managed.

"Lorelei, you sound upset. Is something wrong?" He asked, and she could hear the concern in his voice, and she unraveled.

She hated women who cried excessively, but she couldn't stop the tears from flowing. It took Daniel several minutes of conversation to get her to where she was coherent enough to make any sense. That had been over two hours ago, and things were not looking any better, Lorelei realized, as she sat in the manager's office at her bank in Alexandria.

"We will cooperate fully with the police Mrs. Hannah," John Garcia, the manager, assured her. "We have systems in place that should stop things like this from happening, but the teller assures me a woman came in with a valid driver's license. She was with her husband. She remembered the man making a big deal about this being a fresh start for them both and saying they were moving out of state."

Detective Daniel Sullivan, Danny, to his friends, closed his notebook and stood up. Lorelei did the same even though she was far from satisfied. "I'll be in touch with you, Mr. Garcia, and if your staff remembers anything else, this is my card. I'll be filing a report with the local police. They will handle the case from here on out, but I'd like a heads up if you get any promising leads."

The manager shook hands with Danny, but Lorelei was too numb even to respond when he held his hand out toward her. "Is there anything I can do for you now, Mrs. Hannah?"

Are you freaking kidding me? Lorelei felt like yelling. They'd given all her money to her lying husband, what more could they possibly do?

"I have a check I need cashing," she realized, reaching into her purse for the envelope holding the insurance payout.

"Of course," the manager agreed. Lorelei wondered if there were anything he wouldn't agree to since he knew they'd screwed up royally. She handed over the check, and he blinked at the amount. "I'm not sure we can cash such a large check from another bank."

"You're joking?" Danny's voice dripped with sarcasm. "You let her husband and some random woman close out all of her accounts, and you're quibbling over *this* check?" The manager looked flustered.

"You will cash this check for her because it's from an insurance payout on her car, and you know it will not bounce," Danny was her hero. "Then, you will smile as we walk out that door, and you will start the investigation into how one of your staff members allowed this to happen in the first place." He stopped speaking, and Lorelei watched the manager walk out of the office with the check and her identification. He came back only a few minutes later with a padded envelope and a small stack of bills. He counted the cash for her slowly and put it in the envelope and handed it over. "I promise, I will not rest until I get some answers for you," he said sincerely, and Lorelei believed him.

She had parked the Ranger in the bank's private lot, and Daniel's car was beside it. "I'm sorry you had to take time off work for this," she said.

"I said I'd be there for you whenever you need me. You've had my back many times," he told her, making sure she was safely inside her vehicle with the doors locked and the cash hidden under the driver's seat.

She rolled the window down. "What am I going to say to Beth?" She asked in a small voice.

"Nothing, unless you have to," Danny responded. "Madison has been missing Beth at school, so we'll come up for a day this weekend. The kids can play, and we can start to figure this out."

Lorelei almost managed a smile, but then she saw the clock on the dashboard. "Oh no, I have to pick up Beth in an hour. I don't know if I will get there on time, and it's her first day."

"Don't worry, Lorelei," Danny pointed to the windshield where Toby had attached his EZ-pass. "You can use it on the toll lanes, and you'll make it in plenty of time."

He was right, of course, and she would pay Toby back for any tolls, but the thought of Beth waiting around at school for her made her more anxious than she wanted to admit.

"Thank you for coming to my rescue today, Danny," she said. "I don't think I could have done this without your help."

"Glad I could be of help, ma'am," he said, then he saluted cockily before walking back to his car.

She had people in her corner now, Lorelei thought, and they were people she could trust. Her life was not all bad, she realized as she navigated onto the toll lanes heading south, and by the time she reached the Lake Thomas town limits, she almost believed it.

Jefferson tried telling himself he wasn't waiting for the Ranger to pull back into the lot across the street, but he knew he was just kidding himself. He'd looked for it about a hundred times to no avail.

"She's still not back yet?" Jackson looked up from his desk.

"Who?" Jefferson feigned innocence, but his brother knew him too well to fall for it.

"Okay, full disclosure here, brother," Jackson looked more than a little embarrassed. "I may have witnessed the kiss Lorelei planted on you this morning," Jackson sent him an apologetic half-smile.

"You mention that to anyone else, and I will take you down, little brother, I swear on Mom's grave," Jefferson threatened and was shocked when he realized he meant every word.

Judy Cooper had been the center of their family. But five short years ago, she'd succumbed to pneumonia as a complication of her treatment for pancreatic cancer in a particularly damp and cold winter. "I swear Jefferson, on Mom's grave, I will keep this between you and me," Jackson promised. "So, was that kiss as good as it looked?"

"Dude, seriously, I am not going to discuss anything that has happened between Lorelei and me, so forget it," Jefferson warned.

"*Anything*?" His brother grinned. "I take it that wasn't the first time you kissed her then."

"Leave it alone, Jackson, I'm not talking about this anymore!"

"Don't get your boxers in a bunch," his brother put his hands up in mock surrender. "I was just going to let you know she pulled in across the street and went into the diner with Beth, that's all," Jackson finished smugly.

Jefferson looked across the street, and sure enough, his brother wasn't lying about the truck. "I think we need cookies," he announced, walking out of the door with Jackson's mocking laughter following him.

Lorelei convinced Beth her eyes were red because she was crying over the loss of the PT, which in all honesty had been her favorite car ever. She wasn't sure Beth bought the lie, but she quickly changed the subject to Beth's first day at her new school to deflect any further questions. Her daughter had filled the ride to the diner with stories about her new friend Chelsea and how excellent the cafeteria food was. Lorelei had to blink back tears several times.

"They have a cool library, and it's a separate building. It has tons of books, but the middle school shares it. I got my library card today, and Chelsea likes the same books that Madison and I like," Beth said. She paused for breath finally when they walked in through the back door of the diner, and Lorelei hugged her a little more tightly than usual. "There *is* something wrong, isn't there? Is Malcolm coming here?"

Lorelei usually heard the bell on the front door ring, but not this time. When she looked up, she saw Jefferson standing by the counter. He was looking at them through the open doorway to the back room. "Who's Malcolm, Beth?"

Lorelei didn't have time to say anything before Beth just blurted out the truth. "He's my mother's husband, and I don't like him." She ran to the restroom then. Lorelei was torn between going after her daughter and staying to explain things to Jefferson.

"You're married?" His tone was icy.

"It's complicated," Lorelei began, but he cut her off.

"It's not complicated for me," he said. He took his order from Toby and walked out of the door, without looking back once.

And this awesome day just keeps getting better and better, Lorelei thought, cursing the day Malcolm Miller had ever come into her life. The man had stripped her of her dignity, her friends, her self-esteem, and her daughter's physical and financial security. Now, he'd even ruined whatever was happening between her and Jefferson.

"You go talk to your girl," Toby whispered, sending her a fatherly smile from behind the counter. "He will calm down in time, and you'll get your chance to explain, but right now, your little girl needs you more. Later, we can sit down, and you can tell me all about this *Malcolm*!"

Lorelei felt tears welling up as she headed for the restroom. Beth was leaning on the sink, and she was wringing her hands and rocking back and forth with her eyes closed. "Sweetie, it's all going to be fine. Malcolm is *not* back. He never will be back, but I do have to tell you about what happened today. I was hoping to wait until the weekend, but I know you will just worry yourself coming up with ideas."

"You're not sick like Madison's Mom was, are you Momma?"

"No," Lorelei answered quickly, enfolding her daughter in her arms. She took a deep breath and told Beth everything in the simplest terms she could muster.

"He stole all of our money?" Beth asked when she finished.

"All of the money in the bank, yes. But we have the insurance money from the car, and the bank said we should get all our money back after they complete the investigation, but that will take quite a while. For the moment, we only have a little money," Lorelei explained.

"I hate him so much!" Beth shouted at no one in particular.

Lorelei usually made Beth take back that word, but she wasn't about to tell her not to say it this time. The things she had been calling Malcolm in her head on the drive back from Alexandria would have made a trucker blush.

"He's out of our lives, Beth. We never have to see him again as long as we live!" She promised.

"Amen to that," Toby said from the open doorway. He walked over and wrapped his arms around them. "That apartment is yours until everything gets sorted out, rent-free, and don't argue with me. And you can use my truck whenever you need to. Now, get down to the bank with all that cash and open yourself up a new account. You should get some of that identity theft protection too. There's no telling what that bastard might do if he has someone pretending to be you at your old bank!"

Lorelei hadn't even thought about that. Malcolm had access to her identification, and that was worrying. She looked at her watch; the bank was closing soon, but it was only three blocks away and still on Main Street. "Come on, Beth, let's take a walk to the bank. Our new accounts will make this a fresh start for both of us!"

Jefferson slammed the door of the law offices open with enough force to rattle the plate-glass windows. He hurled the bag of cookies at the wall where it exploded above Jackson's head, showering him with sugar and chunks of dough. "What the hell did you do that for?" Jackson glared at him over his laptop, shaking crumbs out of his hair.

"I'm going for a run," he bit out, heading for the rear door.

"The hell you are, we have too much work to do!" Jackson called after him, but he didn't stop walking until he got to his SUV. He drove off without even acknowledging Jackson standing in the doorway, staring after him with a concerned expression.

He pulled onto Main Street and saw two figures walking on the sidewalk, arm in arm. He knew immediately who they were. He gunned his engine and roared by, making no attempt to rein in his temper. He hoped his brother didn't have a speed trap on Main Street again, or there'd be hell to pay with his Dad for driving like an idiot.

When he got out of the Explorer at his house, he realized it was too cold to run. It was getting dark also, so the only alternative was to grab a beer from the fridge and take it out on the back deck. He hoped the alcohol or the temperature would cool his temper down some.

He'd barely been home for five minutes when he heard cars in his driveway, and then his front door, which he rarely locked, opened, and his brothers stalked inside. Coop glared at him, hands planted on his hips, and Jackson looked seriously pissed.

"You have ten seconds to explain why you were just doing nearly fifty in a twenty-five zone, or I'll haul your dumb ass to jail!" Lucas Cooper warned him.

There was no doubt in Jefferson's mind he meant every word.

"I may also press charges for assault with a bag of cookies," Jackson tried to ease the tension, but it didn't work.

"She's married."

"Who's married?" Coop demanded.

"Lorelei?" Jackson asked. "Are you sure?"

He was sure, Jefferson thought. The guilty look in her eyes had given her away completely when Beth had answered his question.

"Something is going on with you and Lorelei Hannah?"

Jackson opened the fridge and tossed a beer to his older brother and shook his head. "You know you're the sheriff, right? You're supposed to be on top of these things?"

Jefferson closed his eyes at his brother's unfortunate choice of words.

"Shit, sorry, Stephanie's all mixed up in this too," Jackson walked over and wrapped an arm around his shoulders.

"I have one question for you, little bro, and you need to think about this carefully," Coop said. "If she's happily married, why did she load everything she cares about into that little car of hers? Why did she take off with her daughter?"

Jefferson didn't have an answer for that and took a swig of his beer, which brought a sour taste to his mouth he couldn't ignore.

"Follow up question for you, have you noticed how she scans the diner when she walks back out front from the kitchen? Or how she checks the doorway pretty much every time someone comes in?" Coop knew he was onto something.

"Beth said she didn't like the guy, and I was too busy thinking about how this affected me," Jefferson was thinking aloud. He didn't expect his brothers to agree with him, but they did. The front door opened again, and Grace came in, carrying a large covered tray.

"Is this some kind of intervention?" He asked.

Grace looked faintly guilty, and his brothers shuffled uncomfortably from foot to foot. Then Harry Cooper, patriarch of the Cooper clan, marched in.

"Put that beer down, boy. There will be no repeat of the Stephanie *incident* while we're all here to prevent it!" His father commanded.

"I think we have it under control, Dad," Coop laughed.

"Really? He's holding a beer that's been in his fridge for at least two years, and a little bird tells me he drove up Main Street like it was the Daytona 500 not thirty minutes ago," Harry said. "That's what you consider *under control*?"

"This beer tastes bad," Jackson admitted.

Jefferson had realized as much himself. "I will not go off the deep end this time, Dad, I promise you. I think I should have talked to Lorelei before assuming she was like Stephanie. I am a total dick."

"You watch your language around Gracie, mister!" His father warned.

"He *is* a dick, Dad," Grace agreed, and they all dissolved into laughter that gentle, smiling Grace had called him out. She was looking at him now, with a somber expression on her face.

"Spill it, Grace. What do you know that none of us do?"

She paused. "This is in strictest confidence, but I know Lorelei has instructions that some guy called Malcolm

Miller is *not* allowed anywhere near Beth. He's on the list of people who may not pick her up from school. Actually, he's the whole list."

"You need to step away from this for a few days, Jeff, and I have the perfect way for you to do it," Jackson instinctively knew he needed space.

"You want me to fly to LA for the meeting with the Spa execs instead of you?"

Jackson nodded. "I already made a few calls, and it's all set, you fly out tomorrow."

"I think it's a great idea," Harry Cooper agreed. "You need time to think about all this, and while you're gone, we can do a little digging on your behalf."

Jefferson poured his beer down the sink, followed by the others. Who knew beer could go off? He thought, feeling calmer already. He had wanted to break things when he'd driven away from the office, but Jackson hadn't allowed that. He glanced across the room at his brother, who'd grabbed an in-date soda from the fridge. "Get me one of those, please. I need to wash away the taste of that beer."

"Is that Mom's famous Shepherd's Pie recipe in that pan?" Coop asked.

"Oh, yeah!" Grace grinned. "I figured you needed some comfort food."

"Someone lay the table then," Harry growled, and Jefferson walked over and hugged him.

"I love you, Dad," He said sincerely, and then looked around the room at his family. "I love all of you for caring enough to want to step in again."

"We love you too, now enough with the mushy stuff, find me some plates, I'm starved," his little sister ordered.

"And then maybe you can clue the rest of us in on what's going on with you and our newest resident?" Harry smirked, and Jefferson felt his face flush.

"I think I'll just get a few more sodas from the garage," he mumbled as he walked away quickly.

"Need some help?" Jackson called not even bothering to hide his amusement.

"Nope, but remember one day, this will be you, and I will enjoy every second," he called back.

"So, it's like that, is it?" He heard his father say to no one in particular. "I can't say I'm not a little impressed. I didn't think he had it in him."

Jefferson groaned. "I'm in the garage, not the next town. I can still hear you."

Harry Cooper let out a rafter-shaking laugh. "I know you can, son, why do you think I said it?"

Dinner had been over for a few hours, and everyone had left but Harry. Jefferson knew his father had something on his mind.

"Out with it, Dad," he said as they stood on the rear deck. "I know you have something you want to say, so just say it."

Harry Cooper smiled. "You always were the quickest of my boys. Do you know what you're getting yourself into with this woman?"

"She's a good person as far as I know Dad, her little girl is cute, if a little defensive," he began.

Harry cut him off. "Lorelei may be in the middle of a messy divorce; you don't know for sure. The only thing you know is she has a daughter, and that precious little girl should be at the forefront of every decision you make in this affair."

"We are *not* having an affair!"

"Not yet, maybe. But you want to have sex with the woman, don't you?"

"Dad, enough!" He was standing toe to toe with his father, glaring at him.

"I thought so," Harry put a fatherly hand on his shoulder.

"I'm attracted to her. I admit it," Jefferson began, but Harry chuckled. He realized he wasn't fooling his Dad. "I like her a lot."

"Maybe she's the reason you didn't end up with Stephanie?" His father suggested.

"Look, Dad, I know you believe all things happen for a reason, but you might be a little premature about Lorelei and me. We barely know each other."

"True, but do you know how long it took me to fall for your mother?" Harry Cooper asked quietly.

Jefferson shook his head. He knew his parents had met in college and gotten married within a year, but their romance itself hadn't been a topic he and his brothers had much interest in. He was sure Grace talked to their father about their mother all the time, but he tried to avoid bringing her up because losing her still hurt.

"I fell for my Judy the first night we met, at a movie screening on campus. I was with another girl, and she was with another guy, and we caught our dates kissing when we got back from the concession stand," he smiled wistfully.

"Not a great date for either of you, then?" Jefferson said.

Harry Cooper snorted. "We left the movie, and I walked your mother back to her dorm building, and she thanked me for being a gentleman. I realized I wanted to kiss her, so I backed her up against the dorm door. I kissed her like I'd never kissed a woman before or since. She pushed me away and just stared at me for the longest time, and then she asked me if I had a pen to write with and she gave me her number."

"Why are you telling me this, Dad?"

"Because I think you already know Lorelei is important to you, even if you're not ready to admit how important. I wanted you to know sometimes it only takes a heartbeat to fall in love with someone, and they might be *the one*," Harry Cooper stared across the deck, lost in his thoughts.

"What you and Mom had was special, Dad," Jefferson said, reaching out a hand and placing it on his father's shoulder. "If I thought I could have that with Lorelei, I'd consider myself the luckiest man alive. Now, I suppose I'd better pack for my trip."

His father let out another raucous laugh. "And that's my cue to leave!"

SIX

Lorelei woke the next day to pop music and the sound of Beth's off-key singing. All she wanted was to crawl back under the quilt and never come out again, but she knew she couldn't because it wasn't the grown-up thing to do. Being an adult was often overrated, she lamented as she swung her legs out of bed.

"Mom, you need to get dressed and walk me to the bus stop. It's right around the corner, and my teacher told the driver to expect me. Chelsea rides the same bus, too, so you don't have to worry about me at all!" Beth's happiness was infectious, but Lorelei still groaned as she dropped a coffee pod into the coffeemaker. There wasn't enough coffee in the world to make her feel any more awake, but seeing Beth so upbeat made her heart soar. "What put you in such a great mood, anyway?"

"You told me Madison is coming to visit this weekend. And you promised you'd go speak with Mr. Cooper about the whole divorce thing," Beth grinned unapologetically.

Oh God, she remembered making that promise at about eleven the previous night, when she had finally gotten Beth into bed. Although her daughter had fallen asleep immediately, Lorelei had lain awake, fretting about everything. She'd made so many mistakes lately, most notably in the way she'd treated Jefferson, and she didn't want to make any more.

How on earth could she face the man again and tell him she *was* technically still married, but that Malcolm had ripped her off for thousands of dollars? Or tell Jefferson that her husband had put her in the hospital one time too? What kind of woman allowed that to happen to herself and didn't leave immediately? A stupid one! Lorelei chided herself harshly.

Since Cooper Law was the only legal office in Lake Thomas, getting them to handle the divorce made sense. If she could only get up the courage to walk through their door!

Her new bank had been impressive the day before, though, she had to admit. They had opened new accounts, and they'd helped her set-up fraud alerts through online banking and text messages and transaction alerts for her peace of mind. No one would steal from her ever again, she vowed.

Toby had arrived at the apartment just after ten the night before too, holding a pay-as-you-go phone and a top-up card. "It's a gift, so don't argue," he'd told her gruffly.

She'd barely held her tears in check as she'd hugged him tightly. "You are a kind man, Toby, thank you."

After he'd left, Lorelei realized it felt great to have access to a phone number Malcolm didn't know, and she'd thrown her old phone into one of the kitchen drawers.

She spent a few hours tossing and turning in her bed before she'd gotten out of it again and set up the laptop in front of the television and registered her new phone. She changed her contact information at the bank to the newly activated number. Then she went onto Google's website to get a brand-new email address.

Finally, she deleted her old email address, which wasn't as tricky as she had imagined. Malcolm had driven away all her old friends with his incessant checking on her. He'd managed to isolate her from pretty much everyone. Everyone except Ruby and Danny, and he'd certainly tried to get Danny out of the picture too. However, Daniel Sullivan did not kowtow to any man, which Lorelei was eternally grateful for.

"Okay, Beth, I am off to brush my teeth and make myself presentable. Then you can tell me where this bus stop for school is!" Lorelei impulsively hugged her daughter. "We will get through this together because we are strong, independent women!"

Beth whooped with joy and danced her mother around the room, and Lorelei knew this was going to be a good day.

The door into Cooper Law creaked loudly as Lorelei entered as if it were mocking her for her cowardice. The sound didn't altogether drown out the little bell above the door, and Jackson smiled as he came out of the kitchen carrying a coffee mug.

"He's not here," he said, seeing her discomfort, and Lorelei blushed, thinking about the last time she had been in their offices. "Coffee?"

"No, thank you. I wanted to see you," Lorelei began hesitantly. "There's something I need to take care of." Jackson nodded. He already knew about Malcolm and no doubt from his brother, she thought.

"I'm not here to judge you," Jackson said kindly, and she felt tears trickling down her cheeks. The next thing she felt was a muscular pair of arms enveloping her before he guided her to a chair and sat down behind his desk. He nudged a box of tissues closer to her.

"I'm not normally a crier," she began.

"My Mom always said crying was a good safety valve. Maybe you should just start from the beginning?" Jackson suggested.

She hesitated, knowing it wasn't a pretty story.

"Whatever you tell me will be strictly between us, I won't share anything with Jeff unless you give the okay first," he promised.

How had he known what she was thinking? She wondered, then she told him about her marriage to Malcolm, and he listened without commenting once, but his eyes told a different story. She kept quiet about Malcolm beating her, though, that was more than she was willing to share. When she finished speaking, she saw him work his jaw back and forth twice and couldn't help smiling.

"After telling me all that, you can still smile?" He asked.

"Your brother does that jaw thing too," she explained.

Jackson laughed. "True. Our Mom was always pointing that out. It drove her crazy."

"You must all miss her a lot."

"We do, but not as much as Dad and Grace," Jackson spoke softly. "Mom and Grace were best friends. They did so much together. But Dad, he was Mom's rock, right until the day she passed. He did everything for her, and he never let her see how much he was hurting. He fell apart for a few weeks after she died, but then Grace pulled him out of it because she's the one who's most like Mom."

They talked while Jackson filled out the paperwork to begin the divorce process. Then she hesitated, and he was too perceptive. "He flew out to Los Angeles early this morning."

Lorelei blushed. "Am I that obvious?"

He smiled gently. "Neither one of you is particularly good at hiding your feelings."

"I'm not sure I even know how I feel," she admitted.

"That's what Jefferson says too, but I think both of you know there's more than a little something there," he observed astutely. "His ex, Stephanie, burned him badly a few years back, and he hasn't been seriously interested in a woman since. Somehow, you managed to break through his armor."

"Did she cheat on him?" Lorelei couldn't hide her amazement.

"If only he were here to see your face, it would be a huge boost to his ego," Jackson laughed. "And yes, his fiancée cheated on him with his boss and then to add insult to injury, the bitch married the guy too. The whole thing crushed Jefferson."

Well, that explained his reaction in the diner, she thought, he'd been having a major case of déjà vu. He must have thought history was repeating itself in the worst way.

"Is he okay?" She whispered, looking down at her hands to avoid meeting Jackson's knowing gaze.

"We convinced him he shouldn't jump to conclusions, but he'd already figured that much out himself," Jackson stood and stretched his lanky body. Lorelei wondered how his mother had wrangled her three giant sons.

"I know I should have left Malcolm a long time ago, as soon as he started trying to control my whole life. I don't know why I didn't." In retrospect, she could see all her mistakes, but only hindsight was twenty-twenty.

"Jefferson told me he sensed something was off with Stephanie when she worked late so often, but he pushed his doubts aside because he wanted to make it work. I am going to tell you the same thing I told him - it's not *your* fault," Jackson said.

"It feels like it's my fault," she said, although she knew deep down inside his words were true. Maybe it was time to put the past aside. "I think I figured out how they tricked the bank at least. I lost my purse about six months ago, and I got everything replaced. I never could figure out how I managed to lose it."

"You think he stole your purse?"

She nodded. It meant Malcolm had been planning to steal from her for a while, and if he had her license and the woman made herself look like the photo on it, he could easily have passed her off as his wife. When she'd emailed her suspicions, Daniel had agreed. It wouldn't help get her money back any faster, but it would stop her from fretting over how Malcolm had pulled it off. The reason why he had done it was just embarrassing because she knew he must have seen her as an easy mark. But it still seemed like an awful lot of effort for such a small sum of money.

"You look like you want to punch someone," Jackson smiled, clearly amused.

"I'm just mad at myself for being such a fool," she admitted.

"Jefferson was the same. He blamed himself too. He thought he could somehow have done something better, and she wouldn't have cheated on him. He didn't handle it well. He walked out on his job because he couldn't stand the idea of being around them. Then he spent a few months in a dark hole that none of us could drag him out of, so we staged an intervention," Jackson said quietly.

Lorelei smiled, imagining the siblings and their father descending on Jefferson's house en masse.

"Our mom would have yanked him out of his funk a lot quicker than we did," he laughed. "God, we miss her so much."

Lorelei reached out and squeezed his hand, feeling like she understood Jefferson a lot more after talking with his brother, then the phone rang and broke the moment.

"Hey Jeff, your flight got in early?" Jackson winked conspiratorially at Lorelei.

She wasn't really eavesdropping, she knew, but it felt like it, and she headed for the door.

Jefferson was walking through LAX with his carry-on bag and coat under his arm. "Did I hear the bell above the door?"

"Mailman," Jackson replied a little too quickly.

"Lorelei was just there?" He guessed, almost holding his breath waiting for the answer.

"She was, but that's all I can say," Jackson answered, but it was all Jefferson needed to know.

"I'm not asking for any details," he hesitated, unsure of what to say next.

"That's good because you won't get any," his brother told him firmly.

"Just take care of her," he said, before hanging up.

With the phone call over, Jefferson took a cab to The Julius Hotel, which was located a few blocks away from Rodeo Drive. It wasn't his favorite place to conduct business, but one of the spa owners had shares in the hotel, and since they were footing the bill, it was the clients' privilege to choose.

It was an opulent hotel, to say the least, which was the main reason Jefferson didn't feel at home. He was more of a beer and pretzels kind of guy, and this was a champagne and caviar hotel brand. Though, he had to concede they had the best king-sized beds in Los Angeles, and that did count for a lot at his height.

His first meeting wasn't until late the following day. He knew he could take a stroll and explore the exorbitantly priced stores nearby. But, he really wanted to work out the kinks from the long flight in the hotel's pool and perhaps take a siesta.

He was sure he would have missed seeing her in the foyer if he'd had business on his mind, but he didn't. Stephanie Gilbert-Dexter, close to six feet in the spiked heels she had on, was walking away from the front desk and looking directly at him. She smiled, and Jefferson had to check himself before he looked over his shoulder to see who she could be sending that look to because it surely couldn't be him. It was her trademark come-hither look she'd used on him many times in the past, but now it only caused the contents of his stomach to curdle.

"Jefferson, what a coincidence I'm running into you like this! You're not staying at The Julius too?" Stephanie's voice was too loud and overly friendly, almost as if she were trying to make sure as many people as possible saw them together. She tried to kiss his cheek when she stopped mere inches from him, but he turned his head to deflect her. "You're still mad at me, aren't you?" She pouted.

Seriously? He thought, feeling an impotent rage build in his chest. "Mad at you?" He feigned confusion, trying to keep his tone even, despite the churning inside him. "I'm not mad at you anymore, I've moved on Stephanie, no need to reopen old wounds. You have a nice day." He finished speaking and walked away from her toward the bank of elevators. He didn't need to look back to see her expression because he could see her watching him in the reflection in the elevator doors. She did not look happy, he thought, and that caused him to smile.

I'm finally over her, he realized. He'd only felt angry because she'd been so glib about her past behavior, but he'd felt no attraction. Her long black-brown hair was perfectly smooth. Her outfit was undoubtedly some well-known designer or other. As always, her makeup was flawless. Yet, she was a poor substitute for a certain petite blond he'd left behind in Virginia.

It was Sunday again, and a rare April snowstorm was expected within a few hours. Daniel and Madison had planned to stay until late afternoon. Now, they would leave straight after lunch, which they were all having at the Cooper's thanks to Grace's invitation. It was a longstanding tradition for Harry Cooper to host a free-for-all Sunday lunch almost every week, and anyone might be there. Anyone but Jefferson, Lorelei thought, because he was still away on business.

Harry had invited Lorelei and Beth to this week's luncheon. When she'd said they had friends coming into town and couldn't make it, Daniel and Madison were included too.

"Beth, are you ready yet? Daniel will be back with Madison any minute," Lorelei called from the bathroom and almost jumped out of her skin when Beth appeared in the doorway, coat on, ready to go.

"You're like a freaking ninja!" She admonished her daughter, who laughed.

"Can we go visit Madison soon?" Beth asked.

Lorelei smiled. The girls had been playing together all morning while she talked with Daniel about Malcolm. They'd discussed arranging another play date for their daughters too, and they'd come up with a plan. "How about the trampoline place we saw advertised on TV in two weeks?"

Beth didn't answer but jumped around in excitement, so Lorelei was sure they'd made the right choice, plus it was midway between Lake Thomas and Arlington.

The buzzer on the door rang, and Beth went to answer it as Lorelei ran a brush through her curls. She hadn't bothered to put much more than lip gloss on this morning because she hadn't felt the need. Jefferson wasn't due back from California until tomorrow, and she didn't have to impress anyone else in the Cooper family.

When they arrived at Harry Cooper's, Grace opened the front door and pulled them inside. The house was a large two-story colonial. Lorelei could easily imagine the days when it was full of teenage boys and noise. She assumed that was probably why Harry Cooper enjoyed his open-house Sunday's so much. Grace still lived at home, and Jackson lived in an apartment over the detached two-car garage. She knew Lucas had his own place on the far side of town because Toby had mentioned it, and Jefferson lived in his ranch-style home about a mile away. But there was no doubt they were a close-knit family.

She'd never met Harry Cooper before, but she knew him in an instant. He was over six feet tall, like his sons, and graying at the temples. Still, the family resemblance between the Cooper males was unmistakable. She reached out to shake his hand and found hers engulfed before he pulled her into a fatherly hug. "Welcome to our home Lorelei," he said.

He hugged Beth too and Madison and then shook Daniel's hand warmly. "I hear you're a member of the Arlington Police Department?" Daniel nodded, and they walked into the kitchen, talking shop. Grace took Beth and Madison into the family room to watch TV, and Lorelei was left alone with Jackson.

"Are we the only guests this week?" She asked.

"Toby will be here soon, he's leaving the diner in capable hands," Jackson said.

Lorelei smiled. Toby and Harry went way back, although Toby was probably close to twenty years senior to the ex-sheriff of Lake Thomas.

"Jefferson is incommunicado," explained Jackson. "He emailed on Friday."

"Is everything okay?" Lorelei asked, seeing the concern in Jackson's eyes, and he shrugged.

"Lunch will be ready in twenty minutes," Harry announced. "We're just waiting on the roast potatoes."

"I'll see what the girls are up to," Daniel said, heading down to the basement.

After he was gone, Lorelei wandered into the kitchen and watched as Grace and her father worked in perfect harmony. Grace put the finishing touches to a meal for nine. She wondered what it was like to grow up in a family like this one; it was so different from her own upbringing.

Her parents had died when she was so young. She barely remembered them at all, but they hadn't been overly affectionate. Neither had her grandmother who'd raised her after their deaths. Not that she'd felt unloved exactly, superfluous was perhaps a better way of putting it. Her grandmother had taken good care of her. But, she'd been more interested in her own social life than taking Lorelei anywhere with her. When Elizabeth Dickinson had died, Lorelei had felt lonely, but she had grieved little for the woman.

She supposed it was why she had fallen so hard for Joe. He'd grown up in foster care and had no family to speak of, but he'd wanted kids, and he'd loved all the holidays and family outings and school events. They'd wanted more kids and planned extravagant overseas trips. Then he'd worked late one night for some extra cash and gotten into a wreck on the George Washington Parkway and, in an instant, their life together was over.

Lorelei wasn't sure that Beth remembered her Dad because she'd only been three when he died. But, she made sure her daughter knew him from photos, albums, and memory books they'd made together. Whenever Beth asked about Joe, Lorelei tried to remember a different story about him or some small detail that would make him more real for her daughter.

There were memories all over the Cooper house too. Trophies and graduation photos and family memorabilia adorned bookcases and the walls up the stairs and over the piano. Lorelei felt a stab of guilt over feeling so envious of Jefferson's family. It wasn't his fault he'd grown up in a Norman Rockwell painting, but oh, how she wanted that for her and Beth too.

There were photos of Jefferson's mother on the mantle. Lorelei was startled to see the similarities between her and Grace, even though they weren't biologically related. The wedding photo of Harry and Judith Cooper took pride of place on the wall above the fireplace. They were staring into each other's eyes on the steps of a church, and there was no doubt they were head over heels in love.

The sound of a car pulling into the driveway had Grace running to the window. "Toby's here! Oh, it's not Toby," she laughed as she threw open the front door and found

Jefferson standing on the doorstep. "What are you doing back so soon?"

Lorelei felt heat flooding her cheeks and couldn't seem to remember how to breathe when he looked directly at her. She turned and hurried away on the pretext of seeing what Beth and Madison were doing.

Whatever he'd been expecting on arriving home a day early, he hadn't expected to see Lorelei in his Dad's living room. Nor had he enjoyed seeing the look of dismay on her face or the way she abruptly left the room. He was still trying to decide what to do when Jackson walked in through the back door.

"Hey, you're not supposed to be here," his brother said, his tone more serious than Grace liked.

"What is wrong with everyone today?" Grace complained in a peeved tone.

"Nothing's wrong with me," Jefferson countered, looking askance at Jackson.

"Me either," his twin responded, but his eyes were shooting a different message. "Let's take a walk outside, catch up on some work stuff."

Crap, Jefferson thought, somehow his brother had found out about the Stephanie incident at the hotel and was about to give him a whole, heaping pile of grief over it.

Once they were outside, Jackson grabbed his sleeve and dragged him around the side of the house onto the driveway. "Tell me you'd never get back together with *her*, Jeff?"

"What? You think I would actually want to have anything to do with Steph again?" Jefferson couldn't believe his brother could even think he was that weak.

Jackson dragged his phone out of his pocket, unlocked the screen, and opened his text messages. The image that popped up on the screen was graphic, pornographic even, in its content, and it was Stephanie in all her naked glory in a pose that left nothing to the imagination.

"What the hell?"

Jackson was staring at him, sizing up his reaction. "You better explain, and fast!"

Jefferson took a deep breath. He'd been hoping he wouldn't have to tell anyone about what else had happened with Stephanie. What his family didn't know couldn't hurt them, right? So wrong, he thought.

He hadn't realized Stephanie would see his rejection of her flirting as a challenge, but she had. He'd returned from a workout in the hotel's gym on Friday to find someone was in his room. Before he had time to call security, she opened the bathroom door, standing there naked and wet. He'd been dumbstruck at first, and she took that as an invitation. She sauntered across the room, regardless of the open drapes.

"How did you get in here?" Jefferson demanded.

Stephanie pouted as she walked closer. "Don't you want to play with me?"

He hadn't realized he could be so angry and disaffected by a naked woman until that moment. "Get your skinny ass back in that bathroom, Stephanie, and put your clothes back on, then get the hell out of my room."

The ferocity of his words stunned her he could tell. "You'll regret this, Jefferson Cooper, nobody, rejects me, nobody!"

"You have two minutes, if you're not out in the hall by then, security will remove you, clothed or not, I don't give a damn," he growled.

"I hate you!" She spat as she stomped back to the adjoining bathroom.

"Ditto, bitch," he muttered as he walked out into the hall, not even trusting himself to be in the same room with her. It was the first time in his life he'd ever wanted to lay hands on a woman.

SEVEN

"Ditto bitch. You seriously said that?" Coop had joined the conversation partway into the story after pulling up outside the house. He'd held his tongue until the end, but even Jackson was laughing.

"I know, not exactly mature," Jefferson grinned ruefully, glad his brothers believed him.

"That was one hell of a photo she texted," Coop was shrugging out of his jacket, so he could remove his police-issue weapon from its holster for dinner.

Jefferson groaned. "She sent you a text too?"

"Hadn't gotten around to telling him that part yet," Jackson said.

Jefferson's head was still spinning when he noticed Coop looked uncomfortable. Jackson had shoved his hands in his pockets and was shuffling his feet.

"Should I ask how she got her hands on your phone?" Coop asked.

"When I told her to get dressed, I waited in the hall, like a gentleman. Then security escorted her off the premises, and I went back in to pack my stuff, and they moved me to a suite," he explained. His brothers both looked askance at him. "When I went into the bathroom to pack up, my phone was in the toilet."

"You left it in the room with her?" The incredulous tone came from Coop, but Jackson's face echoed the sentiment.

"I'm an idiot, I know. It was on the dresser. I thought she was just spiteful with the phone as a parting shot. I never dreamed she would do something like this."

Coop threw a careless arm over his shoulders. "A normal person like you cannot get inside the mind of someone like Stephanie."

"The hotel kitchen gave me a rice bag for my phone, but I don't know if that helped. I was busy with meetings yesterday, so I just used my laptop. I need to know who else she sent that text to," he suddenly had an idea why Lorelei might be avoiding him.

"All of us for sure," Jackson answered uncomfortably.

If he'd thought he couldn't possibly feel any worse, Jefferson realized he'd been wrong. "Dad? Gracie, too?"

"Yes, but…"

"But nothing. That woman sent my little sister *that* photo," he wanted to rip Stephanie to shreds for putting his family in the middle of her spiteful game.

"Take a deep breath," Jackson said. "Dad and Grace never saw the photo. We were watching TV, and I heard the texts come in, so I went to check my phone, and theirs were in the kitchen too. As soon as I saw the text, I went straight to their phones and deleted it. I warned Coop about it because he was at work."

"You're sure they didn't see it?" Jefferson asked quietly, feeling some of his anger seep away. Both of his brothers were nodding their heads. "Do you think Lorelei saw it?" He could see they didn't know the answer by their reactions.

"You have her number in your phone?" This news intrigued Jackson.

"Yes, I planned to call her while I was away, try to clear the air, but I didn't get around to it."

"Anyone else in there that matters?"

"A couple of college buddies, Toby, the dry cleaners, a few restaurants," he didn't have many numbers on the phone yet. It had been a new phone before its journey into the U-bend.

"She would only send it to people she was sure would upset you or embarrass you. You better hope that rice worked well enough for you to find out who *you* sent that text to."

Lorelei could tell Grace was mad. Jefferson had arrived home a day early, and then he'd disappeared and taken Jackson with him. It was clear they hadn't gone outside to talk about work. "Seriously, what is wrong with everyone?" Grace stalked over to the window and looked outside. "Now Lucas is out there too. What the heck is going on?"

Lorelei didn't know, but Jefferson was giving her time to calm down and compose herself before they served lunch. Just being around the man turned her into a quivering mess of hormones that made her feel sixteen again.

"Here comes Toby," Grace said. "If he joins that group outside, I'll pitch a fit!"

Daniel and Harry walked through from the den, and the girls arrived from the family room announcing the movie was over. The conversation switched to lunch preparations and adding an extra seat to the table. Everyone came in except for Jefferson, and Lorelei knew something was going on. Was he going to skip lunch because she was there? Was her situation making him that uncomfortable?

"Mom, are you okay?" Lorelei found her daughter staring at her, looking concerned, and then she saw Daniel heading her way too.

"Lorelei?" He said, and she could read the question in his eyes.

"Everything's fine," she assured them. "I need to talk to Jefferson before he comes in. I need to explain the Malcolm situation. Is that okay with you, Beth?"

Beth nodded, and Daniel led both girls off to the dining table as Lorelei headed for the front door. She knew she had to face this head-on. There would be no more hiding from conflicts and avoiding difficult conversations. Malcolm was the past, and she was done with him, she told herself, even though her stomach was turning backflips just thinking about what she should say to Jefferson.

He was rifling through a bag in his trunk when she walked down the driveway, so he didn't see her coming. She pulled her cardigan tighter around herself as the chilly wind whipped through the trees. She didn't know what she could say to explain herself, but she wanted him to understand her situation.

It was important to her for him to know she wasn't the kind of woman who jumped from one man to another on a whim and that she rarely reacted to men the way she did to him. In fact, she'd never responded to any man the way she did to Jefferson, not even Beth's father, and she'd loved Joe with all her heart.

She must have made a slight noise on the gravel drive because Jefferson began speaking. "My phone is turning on, but I'm not sure if it will work yet."

Lorelei didn't know what he was talking about, and then he turned, and she could see the surprise in his eyes. "Hey," he said.

Hey? Jefferson thought. He seriously needed to work on his communications skills if that was the best he could come up with. But on turning around and seeing it wasn't one of his brothers behind him, all the breath had left his body so fast he was lucky he'd been able to form even that one word.

"I wanted to talk to you about something," she began.

"You got the text?" He said on a note of resignation, expecting her to be disappointed, angry, or something, but she looked confused. His phone chose that moment to switch on. He scrolled quickly through the text messages he'd sent. He saw six texts from Friday, including one to Lorelei with the infamous porno shot, and yet she looked baffled.

"Did you send it to my old number?" She asked.

"You have a new number?"

She smiled and nodded. "Maybe we should both start at the beginning?" She suggested. "Can I go first? I will lose my nerve otherwise."

He wondered what she was so concerned about, but then he saw her shiver and noted she didn't even have a jacket on. "How about we talk after lunch, somewhere warmer?" He suggested.

She looked uncertain but then shook her head firmly. "I have to do this now because I'm going to lose my nerve," she broke off suddenly, and he saw tears glistening in her eyes.

He didn't know what made him do it, but he stepped forward, opening his coat, and enveloping her in it, pressing her close to his chest. She looked up at him, those incredible blue eyes troubled, and he couldn't stop himself from dipping his head to steal a gentle kiss.

This was *so* not the way she'd expected this to go, Lorelei thought as she stepped back a little from possibly the sweetest kiss ever. There would never be a right time to begin this conversation, so she dove in. "I am still married to Malcolm, Beth's stepfather, at least technically, it's true. But Jackson has started the ball rolling for my divorce. I know I should never have kissed you, then or now, and I know I should have told you right from the start. It was just that you made me feel something for the first time in a long time, and I liked it." Had his cheeks really turned a shade redder than the temperature warranted? She wondered.

"I'm pretty sure we were both involved in all the kisses we've shared," he said.

"But you're not married or even in a relationship with someone, and I am, or I was. I should have made that clear, and I didn't. I'm so sorry, Jefferson," she said and then felt him pull her into his arms again.

"It's okay, Lorelei."

He was so kind, she thought, and she was in danger of totally falling apart, so she took a deep breath and pulled back again. "When I went to deal with my car, I had to take a check from the insurance company to the bank, and

I found out Malcolm had closed all our bank accounts, including Beth's. He took a woman with him, and she pretended to be me. The police are investigating, but I'm kind of broke now, apart from the insurance money."

That was the gist of her story, minus some ugly details about Malcolm assaulting her, she thought, and those could wait for another time. She knew she would have to fill in all the blanks eventually, but it was enough for now.

Jefferson wasn't sure what he'd thought she was going to say, but it had not been this. Her estranged husband had stolen all their money, leaving her with nothing. Gut instinct told him there was way more to the story, but he knew there was something he had to say first. "I'm sorry for the way I reacted when Beth told me about her step-dad. I shouldn't have jumped to conclusions. I should have let you explain. I behaved like a jerk."

Lorelei shook her head. "No, you reacted the way I think most men would. I should have told you after that first kiss."

"That was some kiss," he mused, his eyes turning a smoky charcoal color that had her cheeks glowing. He liked making her blush, he discovered, it made him want to do it more.

He realized it was time for him to bite the bullet on the texting issue. "Do you still have your old phone?"

Lorelei shrugged. "It's probably not charged, but I think it's in a drawer in the kitchen."

"There will be a text from my phone on there. Please, *don't* open it."

"Why not?" She asked in a small voice.

"It's not what you think, and it's not from me. Someone took my phone and sent a text out of spite, then dropped my phone in the toilet," that last part caused Lorelei to cover her mouth with her hand. Jefferson could see she was trying not to laugh.

"My iPhone will never be the same, and you find this amusing?"

"What kind of text did they send?" Lorelei asked, all humor gone from her face.

"*She* sent a photo of herself," he replied, trying to keep the distaste out of his face, but she could read him so well it was unnerving.

"I'm sorry," she said. She reached up and placed her hands on either side of his face and smiled. Jefferson wanted to kiss her again. She glanced over her shoulder and saw his sister at the window again. "Grace looks mad. I think we should go inside for lunch now. I promise I won't look at the text."

He dipped his head to brush his lips against hers one more time before they went inside, and he felt hers soften in subtle invitation before he stepped back. He'd been dreading the conversation, but it had gone far better than he'd imagined. She hadn't even questioned how Stephanie had gotten hold of his phone. She hadn't even asked what the image sent from his phone had been. It made him realize how special she was and just how much she was starting to mean to him.

Lunch was a chaotic, loud affair with the whole family pitching in to serve food buffet style. There was roast beef, chicken, and pork and all kinds of vegetables, sauces, and gravies. If this was a regular Sunday gathering, Lorelei thought, Thanksgiving must be incredible.

They were sitting around the twelve-seater dining table, and everyone was talking all at once, sharing stories and jokes. Lorelei noticed Beth joining in and felt her eyes misting. This was what most families did, she thought, but they'd just had no one to share it with. Jefferson looked concerned. She smiled to reassure him, and their eyes locked and held, and her stomach did a nervous backflip. It took her back to high school when she'd had a massive crush on the quarterback, only the guy hadn't known she existed. Whereas Jefferson was still looking at her hungrily, and his behavior had caught the attention of his brothers, who found it very amusing.

"It's time for some toasts," Harry Cooper announced.

"Hear, hear!" Toby agreed. "I would like to raise my glass to new friends, Lorelei, Beth, Daniel, and Madison!" They held ten glasses up in celebration. She caught Jefferson's gaze lingering on her again, but she didn't hold it this time.

"I would like to offer a toast," she spoke quietly, feeling a little nervous at the sudden silence in the room. She took a slow, deep breath before speaking. "To the deer that stranded us in Lake Thomas, may he live many more happy years!"

Jefferson downed half his glass of wine in deference to the deer that had brought Lorelei into his life. He was finding it hard to keep his eyes off her, and his brothers knew it. They would give him some crap over that later, he was sure. He'd also shared an intense look with Daniel. Lorelei claimed he was just a friend, but Jefferson wasn't sure how Daniel felt. Daniel was not overly tall, but what he lacked in height, he more than made up for in attitude, and it was clear he was very protective of Lorelei and Beth.

Jefferson decided it was time he made a toast and raised his beer high in the air. "To my brother Jackson, for having my back this week." It was a cryptic toast, but Jackson and Coop got the message.

Harry Cooper raised his wineglass before adding, "And to iPads, for receiving duplicate text messages that you will explain later."

Nuts! Jefferson's panicked gaze met his father's stern look. "I can explain."

"You better be able to," Harry responded drily.

Half of the table was clueless; the other was holding their collective breath until Beth stood up and announced she was making a toast too. Lord, make it a good one little girl, Jefferson prayed.

"To my Mom, let's make a toast to a quick divorce from Malcolm!"

Lorelei choked on her wine, and Toby let out a roaring belly laugh. After a few shocked seconds, the entire table erupted into laughter. Prayer answered, he realized, although Lorelei looked mostly mortified, even she was smiling, and there was that enticing blush again.

"Sorry, Mom," Beth whispered as if she'd suddenly realized what she'd just said out loud. Madison looked so uncomfortable it was like she was trying to blend in with the tablecloth.

Lorelei looked like she didn't quite know what to say in response, so Jefferson stepped in to fill the void. "To Beth, for having the guts to voice what most of us were thinking, anyway."

Jefferson found his Dad looking his way approvingly as they raised their glasses high once more.

The table went quiet for a few seconds before Daniel stood up to thank his hosts for a great meal. "We should get on the road before the snow starts, maybe this will be our last snow for this winter!" he said.

Beth and Madison groaned. "Do we have to go now, Dad?" Madison asked, sending puppy eyes her Dad's way, but to no avail.

"Yeah, we do, Maddie. But don't worry, it's not far to Lake Thomas, we'll come to visit again." Madison grinned and ran over to Harry first and then Grace and hugged them both.

Daniel thanked everyone before he and his daughter took their leave. Jefferson walked out to his vehicle at the same time on the pretext of getting something from the trunk. Still, he needed to check with Daniel that he wasn't getting in the middle of something Lorelei didn't fully understand. Madison was already in the car's backseat, settling in with a book and a blanket to combat the unseasonable April weather. Daniel closed the passenger door and looked him in the eyes. "Don't hurt her," he said.

The tone behind the words surprised Jefferson. He'd said the same to Grace's last boyfriend and in the same way. "You and Lorelei never…?"

Daniel shook his head, vehemently. "We've been friends for a long time. Ever since my wife died, since our kids started school together. I never had a sister or a brother either, but that's how I feel about her. She's family to me."

"I won't hurt her," Jefferson promised and reached out to shake the other man's hand. They were just words, but he could read Daniel's promise in the crushing grip he delivered in return.

"Don't," Daniel said simply, before getting into his car and driving away.

They cleared the table and washed the dishes, and Toby went to play table tennis in the basement with Beth, with Lorelei and Grace cheering them on. Jefferson could tell they were having fun by their laughter and knew it was time to talk to his Dad. Jackson, Coop, and his father were in the family room. His father was reclining in his favorite chair, and his brothers sprawled on the over-sized couch, so he flopped down in an overstuffed armchair.

"I can explain the photo, Dad," Jefferson began, but his father waved him off.

"They did that already. I want to know how you *felt* when Stephanie was standing right in front of you, buck naked," his father didn't mince words.

Jefferson didn't know how to answer without sounding like a total jackass. "She was naked, Dad, I'm still a man, and she's still hot. But I never once considered her as anything more than a three-dimensional centerfold."

"So, nothing happened? Nothing at all?"

"Dad, seriously, no, nothing happened. After what she put me through the last time, there's no way I'd ever touch her again. Even if...," he didn't finish the sentence because he heard footsteps coming up from the basement and then Lorelei appeared at the top of the stairs with Grace.

"Are we interrupting something?" Grace asked, picking up on the tension in the room the way only a sister could.

"Just talking baseball," Harry Cooper smiled.

"Well, the Nationals better make it to the World Series this year, it's about time!" Grace commented as she and Lorelei grabbed drinks from the fridge and headed back down to the basement.

"Even if… what?"

His father would never let this go until he heard something to reassure him. "Even if I didn't feel the way I do about Lorelei."

"And how *do* you feel about her?"

"Dad, come on, leave it alone."

"Are you in love with her?" His brothers stopped pretending to watch TV, and all eyes were trained on him.

"I barely know her, and this is my business, not yours," he was trying hard to control his temper.

"You ready to fight me, boy?"

"If that's what it takes to stop you from demanding answers to questions you have no business asking me in the first place, then yeah," he stood up, stalking toward the front door.

"Well, I'll be damned, you were right, Jackson," Jefferson heard his father say, and he turned to see Coop and his Dad handing over a twenty to his twin.

"What the hell?"

"Jackson said you were head over heels in love with the woman. We did not believe him, until now," Harry was grinning unashamedly.

They'd taken bets on him. "I am not in love with…" He was about to deny it, but then he stopped mid-sentence when he realized Jackson was right on the money. "This is too fast, isn't it?"

"What did I tell you about your mother and me?"

His brothers looked curiously at him, but he wasn't going to let them in on that particular conversation. Let them both stew and wonder, he thought. "I'm pretty sure she doesn't know how I feel, and I'm not ready to tell her either."

"Fair enough," Harry agreed. "So long as you admit it to yourself, it's a start."

"You're not going to let us in on the secret about you and Mom?" Jackson asked their father.

"Not until I think you need to know," Harry said, still smiling.

Coop laughed. "Well, on that note, I'm going downstairs to see if Lorelei and Beth are ready to leave, I promised them a ride home."

"If they're ready, tell them I will drive them because you need to get back to work, now that it's snowing again," Jefferson stared his older brother down, daring him to argue.

"Dad wanted to bet a hundred, I talked him down to twenty. You're welcome, Dad!" Coop smirked.

Jefferson turned and saw his Dad was smiling. "It would have been worth a thousand, son."

"What would?" Grace asked as she came up from the basement closely followed by Lorelei, Beth, and Toby.

Something was going on; Lorelei knew the instant she entered the room. Jefferson looked embarrassed, and both of his siblings were trying to hide their amusement. And then there was Harry Cooper, who looked about as smug and self-satisfied as any man she'd ever seen.

"Guy talk, we can't repeat it," Jackson said from the couch.

Lorelei knew instinctively it was something to do with her, but the way they were acting warned her it wasn't something she needed to hear about.

"It just started snowing again," she said to cover the weird mood in the room. "Would it be all right if we went home now?"

"Sure," Coop answered. "But, I have to hand you off to my brother because I need to go do some official police business."

Lorelei smiled, even though gigantic butterflies were flapping around in her stomach. The thought of being in such close quarters with Jefferson again made her giddy like a schoolgirl. Beth would be there, though, so a ride from him should be innocent enough, shouldn't it? She thought.

"Get your stuff together, Beth, you still have homework to do, and there's no guarantee you'll get a snow day tomorrow, the snow might not amount to much!" She said.

"We can always hope, though, can't we Beth?" Toby said with a wink, causing Beth to giggle again. "Would you be able to give me a ride too, Jefferson?"

Lorelei breathed a sigh of relief. Two buffers were more than enough to get through the drive along Main Street, she decided.

Toby was safely inside the diner, prepping meals for the plow drivers for later that evening, and Beth had run straight to her bedroom to finish her homework. Jefferson hovered awkwardly outside Lorelei's front door. He wanted to go in more than anything, but not without an invitation. Judging by Lorelei's expression, she didn't look like she was about to issue one.

"I should go," he said.

"You should," she agreed.

"Do you want me to?"

She shook her head and leaned it against the door with a sigh.

"It was my ex-fiancée who texted the photo," he began. "She was at my hotel in LA, and she got into my room somehow, but nothing happened," he finished.

"Apart from the photo she texted and your iPhone taking a swim in the toilet," she said, fighting a smile.

"It's not funny," he told her, but then she giggled, and he heard his own laughter echoing in the stairwell. "When I thought you might have seen it, I didn't think you would ever believe my side. I thought you might never speak to me again."

"Jackson told me how she hurt you. I can't imagine you would ever let her close enough to break your heart again," Lorelei said.

"I once said I'd let no woman get close enough to me again to tear my heart out," his voice was a soft whisper, but he knew she heard every word. "Never say never." His eyes held hers, her lips parted as she closed her eyes and a single tear escaped and trailed down her porcelain cheeks. He reached over, caught the teardrop on his index finger, and raised its saltiness to his lips.

"I'm leaving now. Not because I don't want to kiss you because you know I do. And not because I don't want to stay because I *really* want to stay. I'm leaving because the next time I kiss you, I want you to be able to kiss me back without reservations or guilt."

She nodded and started to close the apartment's door, but he stopped the door briefly with his foot. "Promise me, you won't look at the text Lorelei."

"I won't," she assured him, and he knew she meant it.

EIGHT

The weeks passed quickly, leading into late April. However, it still wasn't spring-like weather for the time of year in Lorelei's opinion. The snow had melted, but the lake hadn't entirely thawed yet. Lorelei had no hope of fulfilling her friend's final wishes until the temperature improved enough to take a boat out.

She hadn't heard anything from Jackson either, which worried her more than she cared to admit. Hadn't he said he would get back to her soon? She saw him every other day when he stopped by the café to pick up his lunch order, but he didn't say much. Lorelei knew from talking with Grace that they were busy with land sales for the new spa, but surely, she was one of their only divorce clients.

Talk of the devil, she thought as Jefferson walked into King Toby's. His eyes found hers immediately, and he smiled that slow, toe-curling, smile he saved just for her. Oh Lordy, Lorelei felt her cheeks positively glowing. They hadn't kissed since that Sunday when he'd told her about his ex's text. They talked often and texted silly, random thoughts whenever they felt the need. There was a sweetness to their relationship. It almost tempered the physical desire that they both worked so hard to keep in check. *Almost…*

"You didn't call in a lunch order today," Toby called from the kitchen as he caught sight of Jefferson.

"I know, we ate at the spa today, hashing out some final contract details. I only stopped by to invite you both to lunch on Sunday," he said.

"I'm in," Toby grinned happily at the prospect of another Cooper family feast.

"Me too," Lorelei answered. "But Beth is staying over at Daniel's and won't be back until Sunday night."

Beth was having a sleepover, Jefferson thought, and Lorelei would be home alone. Maybe he could convince her to have dinner with him? It would have to be somewhere public because he knew he couldn't trust himself to have her over to his place. Just the thought of her being in his home, her intoxicating scent invading his personal space, was enough to make him need a cold shower.

Talking to her every day without being able to touch her was driving him crazy too. He'd never wanted a woman more, not even Stephanie, but more than that, he needed Lorelei in his life. She made everything seem better somehow.

He loved her, that was the plain and simple truth of it, but he wasn't sure how she felt about him. She had a way of shuttering her expression when their emotions got too intense, and he admired her self-control. But God, it was frustrating because he wanted to know if she felt the same way.

"Earth to Jefferson!" She was smiling, her head cocked to one side in amusement.

"Sorry," he dropped his voice low. "The image of you being alone at your place messed with my head for a moment." He watched her eyes widen in response, and her cheeks flush.

Lorelei saw the humor in his eyes, and her heart flipped over. She turned and hurried back to the kitchen to pick up an order, but she could feel his eyes on her the entire time. She didn't want him to see how easily he affected her, because everything was happening so fast, and yet…

"Have dinner with me on Saturday night. We'll keep it casual, you pick the restaurant, I'll be a perfect gentleman," he promised, mentally crossing his fingers.

"Okay," she answered carefully as she walked back to the counter. Jefferson raised an eyebrow, and she knew her lack of enthusiasm wasn't exactly the reaction he'd been hoping for. “I’m sorry, I’m just worried about the divorce, I haven’t heard anything from Jackson, and I need it to be over.”

“I can talk to him if you want me to?” He was so sweet, and she knew she was all over the place emotionally.

“It’s fine, I’ll stop by the office after my shift. That will give me plenty of time before Beth gets home from school. I’m trying to keep her out of this as much as I can,” she suddenly needed to feel his strength, so she crossed the distance between them to give him a quick hug and stepped back. “I can’t wait to be free of him.”

“I feel the same way, sweetheart,” he said, reaching out to caress her cheek. “I’ll see you in a few.”

Lorelei smiled. He would be there when she saw Jackson this time, and it made her feel better to know he would because her instincts were telling her that something wasn’t right. She didn’t know what it was, but she couldn’t shake the feeling that Jackson would not have good news for her.

“What do you mean, you can’t find him?” Although Lorelei hadn’t wanted him to get involved, Jefferson had just wanted to broach the subject with his brother to get the ball rolling before she came across from the diner.

“Not can’t find him exactly, more can’t find any trace of him, apart from the papers Lorelei gave me,” Jackson explained.

“So, he’s a ghost? He’s just gone?”

"Hell, if I know," Jackson shrugged. "I asked Coop to look into it for me, and he spoke to Lorelei's detective friend, and they're going to get back to me when they know something."

Jefferson felt a gnawing sense of unease in his gut. Maybe Lorelei was right to be worrying about the delay? The worst part was he'd encouraged her to talk to Jackson, and this information was sure to make her feel even worse.

"I have to stop her from coming over here," he said, thinking aloud. "Any ideas?"

Jackson smirked. "I can think of one way."

Jefferson reached out and punched his brother on the arm. "Helpful suggestions only, please. The rehab center still needs office staff, doesn't it?"

"It does," Jackson smiled. "I see where you're going with this, so just stall her by saying the paperwork is held up, but you want to show her something. Take her for a spin in your new wheels. I'm sure they will impress her enough to get in without a fight this time."

"You are *so* funny." Jefferson walked out to the parking lot, amazed that he'd only found Lorelei and Beth stranded on the road into town just a few short weeks ago.

Lorelei didn't even know he'd traded in his SUV for a newer model Explorer and he couldn't help feeling a little excited about her seeing the car. It had all the bells and whistles, as his Dad had put it, with heated seats and a heated steering wheel. Was it so wrong to want it to impress her? He'd been thinking about how it would suit a family one day when he'd bought it. He'd even thought about how comfortable it would be for a little girl to ride in the back next to perhaps one or two child seats. He knew he was getting way ahead of himself, imagining a future with Lorelei and her daughter by his side, but he couldn't help himself. He loved her even if she didn't feel the same way yet.

When Jefferson walked back into the diner right at the end of her shift, Lorelei couldn't stop herself from smiling. "Did you come to escort me across the street, kind sir?"

His response was not what she expected. He walked over to Toby and led him to one side and whispered something, and Toby grinned. What were they up to? She wondered as she grabbed her coat and bag from the rack. She had ninety minutes before she needed to be home for Beth, surely that was enough time to get an update on her situation from Jackson.

"Let me help you with that," Jefferson took her coat and held it up for her to slide her arms in.

"What are you two up to?" She asked, looking from Jefferson to Toby and back again.

"Did you know the Douglas Center is already looking for staff?" Lorelei nodded; Grace had told her the day before. "Did you also know Joyce is ready to come back to work next month?"

Lorelei knew. She'd already checked the want ads to see what was out there, but where was this conversation going?

"We are taking a drive to the spa where I have arranged for you to talk to Victor, the front office manager. They have some receptionist positions that will be available soon," he explained.

"There could be a job there for me?" His words shocked her. Was Jefferson trying to get her a permanent job in Lake Thomas? That meant he wanted her to stay, didn't it?

Jefferson's eyes narrowed as if he didn't know if she were happy or not and she couldn't help herself, she raised herself up as tall as her comfy flats would allow and slid her arms around his neck. Then she kissed him hard, right there in the diner, to a smattering of applause from the regulars. She could tell he was holding back, trying not to respond too strongly. She stepped away and took his hand, waving to Toby as they walked out of the diner together.

"What about Jackson? Should I go see him first?" She asked, but he was shaking his head.

"Jackson said there's no news yet, sorry."

"Oh, more waiting," she was disappointed, but the potential for a new job definitely helped. "I need to change my clothes if we're going to the spa. I want to make a good first impression."

"I'll move my car then," Jefferson said, pushing a button on his keys that activated the locks on the car sitting at the curb. The alarm chirped, and Lorelei looked over at the sleek, black SUV.

"You got a new car?" She asked. His other car had been impressive in her opinion, but this one was downright sexy. She knew she had her mouth open, but when she looked at Jefferson, he was grinning. "What?"

"If I'd known you'd be salivating over my car, I'd have shown you it a lot sooner," he said.

She elbowed him in the ribs playfully and then looked up at him. The look in his eyes made her catch her breath for a moment. "I think you should wait out here while I change, I'll be as fast as I can."

He nodded. "I definitely should, because I won't be able to keep my hands off you if we're alone in your apartment." Lorelei felt her cheeks redden, but she couldn't deny his words were true. It was getting more and more challenging to keep her distance from Jefferson as each day passed.

It was Sunday again, and Lorelei was having lunch with the Cooper's while Beth had her sleepover at Madison's. She'd called Jefferson to postpone their planned dinner the night before, on the premise of having a headache, but she was sure he'd seen through that. It would have been their first real date, but she'd gotten a massive case of nerves. Her life was settling into a pattern of normalcy. He was a big part of that, but being alone with him had seemed like such a huge step. Even in a restaurant filled with people, she knew the only thing she would have been thinking about was sex. Abstinence was torture!

At least Beth seemed to like her new school from what little she divulged to her mother. Lorelei had made the shortlist for one of the receptionist positions at the spa, too, with only one more interview stage to go. Despite Malcolm's disappearing act, her life was moving forward, and it felt good to be in control again.

She watched as Jefferson put the finishing touches on the dining table, smiling at how incongruous his hands looked holding his grandmother's delicate floral china. She caught Grace's eye and knew the other woman was thinking the same thing. They both laughed, causing him to glance their way, his eyes narrowed suspiciously.

"What?"

"Nothing," they said in unison and then laughed some more.

"I'm glad I'm amusing you both," he said good-naturedly as he laid the final place at the table. He turned and walked into the kitchen, closing the distance between them in a few long strides. Lorelei got jittery at the look in his eyes. Would she ever tire of seeing that smoldering need? She wondered. Somehow, she doubted it.

He slipped his arms around her waist, uncaring of Grace watching them. "Look away, baby sister, because I am about to…" Lorelei didn't let him finish his sentence. She slid her arms around his neck quickly and pulled herself up until their faces were level. Then, she brushed her lips over his, running her tongue over his bottom lip until he trembled.

"And that's my cue to be anywhere else but here," Grace muttered, sounding a little flustered.

Lorelei knew she was blushing. There was always someone nearby, like Grace, whenever she kissed Jefferson. She knew she'd never felt this strongly about Beth's father. Joe had been her first love, her best friend, and he'd given her the most precious child in the world, but he'd never affected her the way Jefferson did. Lord help her, she thought, when they finally made it past kissing, they might go nuclear.

"So, I tried to pay Toby some rent out of my paycheck from the diner," she tried to diffuse the tension by changing the subject.

Jefferson laughed. "And how'd that go?"

Lorelei punched him playfully in the shoulder. "You know exactly how that went! He refuses to take any money from me. We've been using his rental place and electricity for six weeks now, and I want to feel like I'm contributing. Still, he won't hear of it after what Malcolm did."

Jefferson's arms tightened around her shoulders as he brushed a gentle kiss across her hair. He still didn't know her entire story, but he knew she was trying desperately to strike out on her own. He could easily help her financially, but that wasn't what she wanted or needed. The job at the spa, now *that* would give her some true independence again.

"You may think you're getting the best end of the deal, but you're an asset to King Toby's," he told her. "I, for one, have been spending a lot more time and money in there lately, and that's good for Toby's bottom-line." He was sure she was the reason there were so many truckers dropping by more often for breakfast.

Lorelei laughed, her chest bumping against his. The woman would be his undoing, plain and simple, he thought. He'd been taking so many cold showers lately, that his water bill would be astronomical. Jackson had also confided in him that the divorce would not be a simple one if they couldn't even find Malcolm. None of that mattered, though, so long as Lorelei stayed.

He looked down and found her looking up at him. "Why are you smiling?" she asked.

"I will have to plead the fifth on that one," he whispered close to her ear, causing her to quiver against him. It was agony, holding her so close, but he didn't want her anywhere but in his arms.

"You two need to get a room," Jackson grumbled as he came through the front door, headed in their direction.

"We will, when you finish the job, she's paying you for," Jefferson responded pointedly.

"Ugh, you two are just too...*everything*!" Grace complained as she returned, carrying a plate of biscuits to the table, but Lorelei caught the smile she was trying to hide.

"We should have a little more decorum," she breathed.

Jefferson wanted to reassure her, but then his father and Toby walked back into the room.

"Don't listen to these grumpy, single, curmudgeons. They're just jealous because you've found something, they both wish they had," Harry proclaimed. "I am glad you have each other, and I am glad to have you and your darling daughter here with us!"

"Hear, hear!" Toby echoed.

Jefferson felt the hitch in Lorelei's breath. "Hey, don't cry," he whispered, trying to comfort her. He looked over her head at his father, panic in his eyes, and found his Dad grinning back at him. Jackson was smiling too, and Grace's eyes looked as misty as Lorelei's. "You guys are no help at all."

"You don't need help, son, you're exactly where you're meant to be," his father told him gently.

Lorelei took a deep breath in to compose herself at precisely the moment Coop opened the front door, removing his hat and jacket. "I hope dinner is ready, I'm starved, and I've been working a twelve-hour shift. What did I miss?"

As Lorelei and Grace hurried into the kitchen in response to the oven timer's insistent beeping, Jefferson shrugged, but Coop laughed. "I don't need any updates on you two, it's plain as day what's going on there."

Jefferson was happy to take the good-natured ribbing of his family, but not if it might make Lorelei uncomfortable. "She's off-limits from now on."

Three pairs of eyes turned on him, and he knew he was drawing a line in the sand he'd once drawn before. They had respected that line with Stephanie, although she'd never tried to fit in with the family. He knew they would do the same and more for Lorelei and her daughter, but this time it meant more to him because *she did*.

"Only until her issue with her husband gets sorted out," Jackson clarified. "Then, she's fair game."

"Deal," Jefferson agreed. The sooner her husband was out of the picture, the better, he thought.

Lorelei and Grace cleared the table after lunch, and the men washed the dishes, giving Lorelei her first chance to ask Grace how Beth was doing in her new school.

"She's doing fine," Grace said. "She's made at least one friend, and she looks happy at recess whenever I'm there to supervise."

Lorelei smiled in relief. She felt like Lake Thomas could be their new forever home, and she desperately wanted it to feel the same way for Beth too. It hadn't been hard walking away from her marriage or Malcolm. Still, it had been difficult to separate her daughter from the only home and school she could remember and her best friend. If Beth was feeling more settled, she thought, then maybe Harry was right, and everything had happened for a reason?

"You haven't mentioned any friends in Alexandria, apart from Daniel," Grace said curiously.

There was a good reason for that, Lorelei thought. "Malcolm disliked all of my friends, and he wasn't shy about letting them know. Eventually, they all stopped emailing and calling, and I suppose I stopped caring."

"Wow, he sounds like a real jerk," Grace clapped a hand to her mouth as the words came out. "I'm so sorry, that was totally tactless, I shouldn't have said it."

"Don't worry, he was a jerk, and I was an idiot to stay with him for so long. He couldn't scare away Daniel, though, or Ruby," Lorelei said.

"Ruby, that's such an unusual name," Grace said.

Lorelei smiled. It *was* an uncommon name, and Ruby had been one-of-a-kind, like the gemstone she was named for. She hadn't liked Malcolm from the outset, and she'd never warmed to him. She'd only been a friend for a few months before he'd come onto the scene. I should have listened to her, Lorelei thought, but that was over with now. Malcolm was gone, and Ruby was finally at peace. Once the weather improved, she could scatter Ruby's ashes on the lake as her friend had requested.

"Time for some coffee!" Harry announced, carrying in a tray.

"Irish, I hope," Toby winked.

"For you, of course," Coop said. "You can always walk home."

Grace grabbed two coffees and brought them over to where Lorelei was now sitting on the sofa next to Jefferson. "I've only ever heard the name Ruby once before," she said to Lorelei and then looked horrified as Toby glanced her way. "I'm so sorry Toby, I wasn't thinking at all."

Lorelei didn't understand what was going on, but the usually unflappable Toby looked disconcerted. "It's her birthday tomorrow, you know. She's turning fifty-two."

Lorelei choked and then went pale. It couldn't be, could it?

"Are you feeling okay?" Jefferson's concern was evident.

"Could we get some air?" she asked, smiling apologetically at the others.

"Ah, some alone time for the lovebirds," Toby quipped.

No one seemed to think it was unusual for them to want to go outside even though it wasn't a warm day. They didn't take their jackets because Lorelei was practically dragging Jefferson out the back door to the small enclosed area overlooking the garden.

Something was wrong, Jefferson didn't know what, but he could feel the raw emotion coming off her in waves. "What is it, Lorelei?"

"Who was Toby talking about?"

"His daughter," he explained.

"What happened to her?" She asked.

Jefferson shrugged. "No-one really knows. The official line is that she ran away from home just shy of her eighteenth birthday. Toby hasn't heard a word from her in over thirty years." After he finished speaking, she looked even more upset. What the hell was going on?

She took a deep breath. "Malcolm drove away all of my friends by acting up. Only two of them stuck around. One was Daniel, and the other was my friend Ruby. After she died, I knew I had to leave."

Jefferson waited. The other shoe was about to drop, figuratively, he was sure.

"Ruby's fifty-second birthday would have been tomorrow," Lorelei finished.

Shit!

"It could be a coincidence," he said. But it would be one hell of a coincidence that two women named Ruby would have been born on the same day of the same year and presumably in the same geographical area. Lorelei still looked upset, and he could tell there was more.

"She asked me to scatter her ashes on Lake Thomas after she died, that's why I came to town in the first place. She said the lake was her favorite place to go when she was a girl," Lorelei finished quietly.

And the other shoe hit the floor! Jefferson had to admit the evidence was conclusive.

"I don't know what to do," she whispered, looking up at him from her seated position in the gazebo.

He joined her on the bench, wrapping an arm around her shoulders. "You sit here for a few minutes while I go get my Dad. Toby is his best friend, and he handled Ruby's disappearance in the first place when he was still a deputy, he'll know the best way to approach this because I sure as hell don't have a clue."

Neither do I, Lorelei thought. She was in shock. Could it be that her friend of just a few short years was Toby's runaway daughter? The dates all lined up too neatly, and Ruby's final wish had been for her ashes to be scattered on

Lake Thomas. Could there really be any doubt who she was? Her last name hadn't been King; it had been Clements, but then she might have been married or changed her name for some reason.

Ruby might be Toby's daughter, Lorelei could hardly believe it. Yet, Ruby was so like him, always taking care of others even though she was the one who had terminal cancer. They'd met through Lorelei's church's volunteer group at the cancer center. Ruby had been the one to comfort her when Malcolm's behavior went from bad to worse. She'd even been there at the hospital the night it had escalated. Lorelei remembered that night so well because of Ruby's kindness.

"You need to leave him," Ruby said. "Before he does something worse than this to you and your little girl."

Luckily, Beth was at Daniel's on a sleepover that night. Lorelei had only called Ruby because the hospital wouldn't let her go home alone with two cracked ribs, stitches, and a black eye. She couldn't tell Daniel the truth because then Beth would find out. She couldn't say anything to him because she knew he would go after Malcolm himself, and she didn't want anyone else's life to be ruined by her mistakes.

When a police officer arrived in the ER, at the request of one of the nurses, she'd lied and said someone had tried to mug her, but she didn't see who it was. She knew the police report would go nowhere because she had provided no details they could follow up on, but she hadn't done it for Malcolm's sake. Malcolm had moved out two days after the incident, so she'd lied to Daniel. She'd said she was home alone when she'd fallen down the stairs at the apartment building.

Ruby had sat with her all that night, helping her plan her escape. Then only a week later, her friend had relapsed because of an infection. She'd spent the next two weeks in the hospital, fighting for her life, a battle she would ultimately lose.

Malcolm was still on the extended business trip she'd invented to explain his prolonged absence. It was the excuse she had used for why he never made it to the memorial service, enabling Lorelei to execute Ruby's plan of escape. But, it had taken a few weeks to fully implement it. She had no idea where he really was during that time, they'd barely spoken after he attacked her and she was glad.

The door to the yard opened then, and it jolted her out of her memories. Harry Cooper came out of the house alone. It was clear from his expression Jefferson had apprised him of the situation. Jefferson was standing on the other side of the glass door, talking to Coop, probably letting him know too, but he turned and sent her a reassuring smile.

"Well, this is an unexpected turn of events," Harry said. "Do you have any photos of your Ruby, so we can compare?"

"On my laptop, and I think I backed them up to the cloud, too, I should be able to log in here if you have a computer I can use?" Lorelei said.

"You knew my Ruby?" Toby asked after looking over the photos she'd accessed via Harry's iPad.

"She was a friend of mine. I met her when I became a volunteer at church. We would go visit people having cancer treatment and give them rides," Lorelei explained. "I met Ruby during her second round of chemo."

They were in the living room alone as everyone else had gone to the basement to give them some privacy. Lorelei perched on the edge of the armchair, and Toby sat down shakily in it, with his elbows resting on his knees.

"Did she suffer?" Toby's anguish was palpable, his body seeming to shrink under her gaze.

Lorelei's eyes filled with tears. "She was tough, right until the end. She was still giving me advice right before she…"

Toby cracked then, dropping his head into his hands and sobbing. Lorelei sat beside him and wrapped her arms around him and held on tight until his ragged grief calmed. A few weeks ago, she hadn't even known him, she thought. Now, she would give anything to take away the pain he was feeling - the suffering she had brought on him, however, inadvertently.

"I'm so sorry, Toby. She was my friend, and she asked me to come here to scatter her ashes after she died. That's how I came to be in Lake Thomas in the first place. I think she sent me here to find you. I feel like she was my guardian angel," Lorelei whispered.

He grabbed onto her hands then, and she felt him nodding. "She didn't have a husband, then?"

Lorelei shook her head. "She never spoke of having any family at all, I'm sorry. I got the feeling she had a lot of regrets, but she didn't talk about her past. I wish I'd known who you were from the start."

Toby lifted his head then and smiled at her sadly. "Me too, but now you really are part of my family because I know she sent you here. We needed to find each other. We need to heal together."

"We do," she said. "I don't plan on leaving any time soon, either. I like it here, and so does Beth. She has no grandparents, so we would love it if you would fill that gap for her. Ruby was family to us, and now, so are you."

"I adore that little girl of yours, I'd be honored," he said proudly.

"Beth loves you too," Lorelei said. "So, do I. You've been so kind to us and done so much for us, I can see where Ruby got it from. You helped us when we needed it, and we will help you get through this." She hesitated for long enough that Toby noticed.

"There's something else?" He asked.

"She asked me to scatter her ashes on the lake," Lorelei told him.

"On the lake?"

Lorelei nodded. "I haven't gotten around to it yet, but I think you should do it."

"I scattered her mother's ashes there, they both loved to go to the lake when Ruby was a child. We should do it together. We can take a boat out, as soon as it's warmer," Toby reached for her hand and squeezed it.

"I think Ruby would have liked that," Lorelei agreed.

A movement behind them made her realize Harry had returned from the basement, and he was holding two glasses and a bottle of whiskey.

"I think this is my cue to get on home before Beth arrives back from her sleepover," she said. "And I think someone else wants to join you."

She stood and was on her way to get her coat when Harry placed the glasses and bottle down on the side table and reached out and engulfed her. "You are family to all of us, Lorelei, now and always. Remember that."

NINE

It was still the talk of Lake Thomas, Lorelei thought. More customers than usual were coming into the diner on the pretext of ordering coffee and cookies. But, they were really coming in to hear more about Ruby and how Lorelei fit into the story. Toby was taking the attention as well as he could, but she knew it was taking a toll on him.

Local morning shows kept calling Toby to see if they could do a human-interest story too. Lorelei had heard Toby say no repeatedly, but they never gave up. Ruby's disappearance had been big news at the time.

"I'm sorry I brought this on you," Lorelei reached for Toby's hands, and he held on tightly.

"You gave me peace," he said, but she shook her head in denial. "I mean it, my dear, you don't know the thoughts that have gone through my head over the years. Now I know she lived her life. I wish I knew why she never came home to us, especially when she was so close, but at least she wasn't dead in a ditch somewhere. You brought me the blessing of knowing."

Lorelei had never thought of it that way before. If Beth went missing, she couldn't imagine what it would be like, not knowing if she were alive or dead.

Grace came into the diner then, her usual smile muted. Lorelei knew it was because she, too, was feeling Toby's pain. Grace had been the biggest news story to happen in Lake Thomas until now. Being abandoned in the back seat of a police car seemed far more dramatic to Lorelei. But, Ruby's story was now the hot topic again as far as the press was concerned.

"How is he doing?" Grace whispered, sliding into her usual booth.

"He took a whole week off, and he said, that had to be enough," Lorelei looked over her shoulder to where Toby was bustling about by the espresso machine. "I wish I knew why Ruby wouldn't come home, I feel like I brought him the worst news ever and left him with so many unanswered questions."

Grace reached out and gave her hand a squeeze. "I know you feel to blame, but it's not your fault. I may have a way you can take your mind off it for a while, though."

Lorelei was intrigued. "Does it involve sewing?" She asked.

Grace laughed out loud. "God, no. Why would you think such a thing?"

"I keep hearing people talk about the summer craft festival, and I thought maybe there was needlework involved." Lorelei grimaced; sewing was her nemesis.

"You know, you are partly right. We are short on volunteers for the festival in June. We need help with organizing. We have plenty of booths, food trucks, and craft sellers. We just need people to help with publicity, set up and decorations," Grace shot her a fake smile and batted her eyelashes.

Lorelei couldn't help laughing. "Do you ever *not* get your way?"

"Rarely. I'm very persuasive. If you ever need lessons, just ask."

"I'm in," Lorelei agreed. Being involved in the town's events would be a great way to get to know more people, and it would provide a welcome distraction from everything else in her life.

"We're meeting at the school library on Friday at seven. You're welcome to bring Beth," Grace rose from the booth, and Lorelei planted her hands firmly on her hips in mock indignation, earning a rueful grin from her new friend. "Yes, I really did just come in here to hit you up to volunteer, I am a terrible friend and a worse customer." Before Lorelei realized what was happening, Grace reached out and gave her a warm hug. "I've got to go and Shanghai my friend Karen now, she didn't help last year because her sister got married, but this year she has no excuse. See you Friday!"

Lorelei was still smiling as she walked into the kitchen. "She got you, didn't she?" Toby smirked.

"You know her too well. I am apparently volunteering for the Lake Thomas Summer Festival, although I'm not really sure what it is," she shrugged.

"It's an excuse for people to get together, eat a bunch of fried food, and enjoy each other's company. We have four festivals a year. This isn't even the best one, but it's fun," he chuckled, seeming like his old self again.

"Four?"

"Music festival in August, fall festival when you'd expect it, and the best one is right before the end of the year, and Beth will love it, she might even be in it," he explained. "Ruby used to be in the Christmas one every year until she went to high school. We have a concert, followed by a dance and buffet. It's at the school, just like the June Festival, but it's inside. There's a Christmas market too where the kids can shop for little things for their families and visit Santa. We decorate Main Street too."

It sounded beautiful, and she couldn't wait to tell Beth all about it when she got home from school. She felt surer every day that Lake Thomas was the right place for them to call home. The people were kind and neighborly, and she'd found new friends.

Malcolm was the only fly in the ointment now, and how far could her money have taken him, anyway? She wondered. It wasn't as if she'd had a lot. How did a man disappear so entirely on so little?

Jefferson couldn't believe he was playing poker with his Dad on a Friday night, instead of spending time with Lorelei. Except that Lorelei was volunteering for the upcoming festival, leaving him with no excuse to avoid the game. It was never really about poker either. It was his Dad's version of a book club. Toby and Harry caught each other up on local gossip, drank fine Irish whiskey, and occasionally played some poker.

When Grace walked into the kitchen a few minutes before seven, he saw his chance. "How about I come by the school and help out too? Another pair of hands wouldn't hurt, right?"

"Oh no, that's not happening, big brother! You and Lorelei are a distraction for each other, and I'm going to make sure I keep you separated, for the sake of the festival!" Grace hugged him, and he was sure it was partly to let him know she was just ribbing him.

The doorbell rang, and Toby let himself in, followed by Coop, Jackson, and Daniel Sullivan. He wasn't sure why the latter was there, but judging by the man's expression, it wasn't for a friendly poker game.

"You have news, I assume?" Jefferson asked.

Grace punched him on the arm. "Have you ever considered you could let someone take off their coat before grilling them?"

Daniel took the hint and removed his overcoat, and Grace hung it in the closet. Jefferson watched him take a deep breath as if he were trying to compose himself. He didn't know Lorelei's friend well, but he looked like he wanted to punch something.

Jefferson watched as Daniel took a Manila folder out of his inside jacket pocket and handed it to his Dad. Harry Cooper frowned, opened the file, and flicked through its contents, then he did something he rarely did. "Son of a bitch."

Coop was looking over their Dad's shoulder, his expression grim, and then Toby leaned over, and his mouth took on a thin, sad line. "What are you looking at?" Jefferson demanded.

Grace was putting on her coat, but at his tone, she turned to them. "What is it, Dad?"

"I need to see what's inside that folder," Jefferson demanded, holding out his hand.

Daniel handed it over, and he opened it with Grace at his side. They gasped in unison. The folder contained a police report of a woman who'd been beaten and photographs of her bruised face. She had a half dozen stitches by her right eye, and it was half-closed. She had a swollen jaw on the left side. The report stated that an unknown assailant had mugged the woman, but Jefferson was sure he knew who had done this to Lorelei.

"You let this happen to her!" Grace, normally so amiable, jammed her finger into Daniel's chest hard enough to force him to step backward.

Harry stepped between his daughter and the object of her anger. "Grace, you need to take a breath. We don't know the full story here."

Jefferson watched his sister turn on her heel and march towards the front door, where she paused. "What kind of detective are you to let him do that to her and get away with it? You should be ashamed of yourself." And with that parting shot, she slammed out of the house.

"What's the real story?" Jefferson asked, knowing there was more.

Detective Daniel Sullivan flexed his shoulders angrily, cracking his neck. "Lorelei told me she got in an accident. Beth was with me that night on a sleepover with Madison. I believed her because she'd never lied before, I had no reason to think she was lying then. I should have realized something was wrong when Malcolm left on a business trip right after it happened."

"How did you find out?" Toby wasn't the only one who wanted to know, but he was the first to find his voice.

"There were fingerprints on some of Lorelei's stuff that's in storage. She gave me a key to the place and her post office box, too," he began. "Your brother lifted her prints from a wineglass when she was here for lunch. Lorelei and Beth's prints were all over their stuff, so it was easy to rule them out. Then there was another set I ran and matched to several open fraud cases and two assaults under various aliases," Daniel paused. "The mugshots I saw were all Malcolm Miller, just with different hairstyles and names. There's never been enough evidence to make a strong case in court, but it did make me question what Lorelei had told me about her accident, so I back-tracked and found this report."

"Bastard!" Coop ground out. "No wonder she left him."

Everyone agreed, but Jefferson was in a different place. Malcolm had beaten her so severely she had needed to go to the emergency room. All this time, she'd kept that to herself. "She was trying to protect you." All eyes were on Jefferson after he spoke, including Daniel's.

"He's right," Coop said. "Any of us would have beaten the living crap out of that guy for what he did to Lorelei. She knew you would have too, and she didn't want that."

"That all may be true," Daniel said. "But your sister was right. What the hell kind of detective am I that I missed this?" He pulled out one photo and slammed it onto the poker table. Lorelei's battered face stared back up at them. Jefferson pieced together another part of her story, which explained a lot.

Grace was setting up worktables at the library when Lorelei arrived with Beth in tow. Beth sent Grace a quick wave as they joined the group of volunteers chatting by the refreshment table. Grace seemed out of sorts, distracted, Lorelei thought, but maybe she was projecting her own feelings onto the woman? She felt a little jumpy about meeting so many new people herself, maybe Grace was nervous too?

With Beth occupied on a computer playing Minecraft, Lorelei threw herself into the meeting. She came up with ideas for decorating and volunteered to help put up posters. It was another way to get to know the town, she realized, and the exercise wouldn't hurt either.

She got to know Libby, the woman who ran the coffee shop at the campground and found out they held summer camps every year that Beth might enjoy. She met Rupert, the man who handled most of the landscaping in town and recognized him as one of Toby's regulars. Beth's teacher, Gloria Evanston, was there too, and the town's mayor and one of the deputies who worked with Jefferson's brother. She was sure his name was Artie, and he came into the diner for breakfast most days. It was nice to put some names to the faces she saw so often, she thought.

Karen was there too, and Lorelei realized Grace had managed to coerce her friend into helping this year. She should be in politics, Lorelei thought with a smile, there didn't seem to be anything or anyone that could stop her.

The meeting ran for two hours. Everyone signed up for multiple projects for the festival that was less than two months away. The only person who didn't seem enthusiastic was Grace. She volunteered for more than anyone else, there was just something not quite *Grace* about her.

Once everyone else left, Lorelei asked Beth to finish up her game and made her way over to where Grace was wiping down the conference table. "Are you okay?" She noticed the other woman's hand shook a little as she paused in her clean up. "Grace? What is it, what's wrong? You can tell me."

Grace put the cloth down carefully and turned to her, with tears in her eyes. "I know about Malcolm, what he did to you. I'm so sorry Lorelei, he should never have treated you like that."

Lorelei inhaled unsteadily and looked over her shoulder to see if Beth was still playing her game, and she was. "What do you know?"

"I saw photos of you in a police report," Grace looked uncomfortable.

"Who showed you the photos?" Lorelei asked, her mind reeling as she tried to piece together how her shameful secret had gotten out.

"Your friend, the detective showed up at our house tonight with the report."

At the words, Lorelei felt her carefully reconstructed self-image shatter into a million pieces and then slowly try to put itself back together.

"Danny *knows*?" she croaked. "Who else?"

Grace looked at her in shock. "Crapola, Daniel didn't know about this, did he?" Lorelei shook her head, and Grace covered her face with her hands.

"What happened between you and Daniel?"

"He was at our house. He had a folder with a police report. I told him he should be ashamed of himself for letting that happen to you," Grace peeked out from between her fingers. "Basically, I told him he was a lousy detective."

Lorelei laughed, then stopped herself, then started again, and then she let the tears fall because she didn't have the energy to stop them. Grace reached out and wrapped her arms around her, consoling her as Beth ran to her, looking scared. "Your Mom is fine, she got a little upset thinking about all the stuff you've been through lately," Grace whispered.

"I know it's about Malcolm, isn't it?" Beth's anger exploded. "If he ever hurts you again, Mom, I will kill him. I will!"

Both Grace and Lorelei stared down at Beth. "You knew?" Lorelei whispered. "I'm so sorry Beth, I thought I'd done such a good job of hiding it from everyone."

Beth frowned. "I saw his hands when I came home from my sleepover. He had scrapes and bruises on them, and you didn't look like you fell down the stairs. I knew he must have hit you, and I promised myself I would never leave him alone with you ever again, and I never did."

It was true, Lorelei realized. Beth had been her shadow after her trip to the emergency room. She'd thought it had been because her daughter's father had died in an accident and she was scared the same thing could have happened to her mother.

"You are the best daughter a mother could ever have, but you never have to protect me from him again. From now on, it's my job to protect you!" she promised, kissing Beth's head gently as she tried to process everything that Grace had shared.

"It's my job to protect both of you from now on," a deep voice echoed. Jefferson was standing in the doorway to the library, looking solemn.

She could feel his anger simmering just below the surface, but before she could form any words, Beth left her side and ran to him, wrapping her arms around his waist in a death grip. "You mean it, you promise?" she asked, the words muffled by his coat, and Lorelei met his eyes from across the room. She watched him place a gentle kiss on the top of her daughter's head, just like she had, then he whispered something in her ear.

"I swear on my mother's grave, I will protect you both," Jefferson promised. Beth hugged him like her life depended on it, and he felt something come over him he'd never felt before. He felt a momentary flash of panic at the intensity of his desire to protect this child from harm. This feeling was probably something parents felt every day of their children's lives, he acknowledged. How had his Dad done it so many times? He knew he and his brothers had been hellions as teenagers, even though Grace had been a sweetheart. Harry Cooper deserved a freaking medal for all the crap they'd put him through.

Beth pulled away as his sister walked over. "I'm never going to be able to look him in the eyes again."

"Don't worry, Daniel didn't blame you for what you said. He was beating himself up pretty badly for the same reason," he reassured her, chucking her under the chin the way his Dad would have.

Lorelei gathered her coat and bag, and he could see she was struggling to regain her composure. She looked shaken up. He didn't want her to go home alone, but he didn't want to crowd her either.

"You could come home with me tonight, Lorelei. I have two extra bedrooms. We can watch movies, play video games, pig out on pizza." He was holding his breath. He didn't want her or Beth to be alone. But mostly, he needed to hold her in his arms and keep her safe. Despite his best efforts to oust it, the image of her battered face kept coming into his mind.

She bit her bottom lip, and her eyes looked haunted. Beth hurried over to her mother and buried her face in Lorelei's scarf. "Can we go to Jefferson's?" She asked. "Please?"

"Is that what you want, Beth?" Lorelei smiled down at her daughter, blinking back fresh tears. Beth nodded enthusiastically.

"Can you drop us at the apartment to grab a few things and pick us up again in about half an hour?" Lorelei asked.

"Sure," he agreed, trying to hide his relief. "That will give me time to go buy junk food at the pharmacy and for Grace to get her stuff together because she's coming to the sleepover too."

Jefferson dropped them off, and Lorelei watched happily as Beth ran into the apartment and straight to her bedroom and threw things into her backpack. Her daughter was excited about the impromptu sleepover at Jefferson's house, which must mean she liked him. It made

Lorelei's heart happy to know her daughter hadn't been scarred for life by her poor choice of husband.

Like almost everyone else, Beth had been charmed by Malcolm at first, because he'd been kind to her. But after the wedding, it hadn't taken long for him to show his true colors. His temper was always on a short fuse when he didn't get his own way, and the romantic gestures of their courtship had vanished. It was as if the marriage had been his goal, and once it had been achieved, the real Malcolm surfaced.

Jefferson was nothing like him, Lorelei thought gratefully, but everything about their relationship was happening so fast. Was she making the same mistake again, moving too quickly? She didn't think so, but her emotions were whirling like she was caught in a tornado. Could the feelings she had for him be the genuine happily-ever-after kind of thing? Could it really happen so quickly?

She walked into the bedroom and over to the closet to get out a duffel bag for the night. As she reached for the door handle, she paused. Was it her imagination, or had the closet seemed to shimmer, like the horizon on a hot day? She pulled her hand back from the metal handle and held her palm close to the door. She felt warmth, and she was sure she smelled the faint odor of burning wood. There was a fire somewhere in the building. Her best guess was that it was on the other side of the wall beyond her closet, which adjoined the apartment next door.

Lorelei hurried back to the living room. "Beth, I don't want you to panic, but I think there's a fire. We have to get out right away!"

Her daughter rushed back into the room. She was ready to leave for the sleepover with her backpack on her back and headed for the front door. "Stop!" There was a haze over there too. "I don't think we can risk opening that door." The smell of smoke was steadily getting stronger, and all her doubts were gone now; the building was on fire.

The apartment windows were large, and she saw no evidence of smoke or flames in that direction. It was their only safe way out, but it was about a twelve-foot drop to the street. They might break a few bones, she decided, but they wouldn't die from the fall, and it was their only viable option. She ran to her bag, grabbed her cell phone, and dialed 911 just as she heard smoke detectors begin blaring on the floor below.

She gave the operator the address in a calm, level voice, then she handed the phone to Beth. "Stay on the line with her, Beth!" she instructed, knowing that if her daughter kept talking to the operator, it would help keep her breathing under control.

She dragged the sheets off her bed just in time to see a darkening patch on the drywall growing larger by the second. Her breath caught in her throat as she felt her first moment of panic. The fire was coming through from next door, she realized, there was no time to waste.

She was halfway out the door when she remembered her keepsakes box. It contained all the photo albums and precious memories from Beth's life and personal papers too. She knew it was in the dresser by the window, and she sprinted to it, almost pulling the drawer out. Holding the pink cherub box securely under her arm, Lorelei ran out of the room, closing the bedroom door just as the flames broke through from the apartment next door.

"Mom, the lady on the phone says we have to find a way out, right now!" Beth half-sobbed, half-coughed. Smoke was seeping into the main room now, and Lorelei knew it was affecting her daughter's lungs. She dragged the sheets over to the window as quickly as she could, taking the phone from Beth when she got there.

"Hi operator, I don't know your name, but we are going out the window now," she said. The operator agreed, advising her to tie off the sheets at the top and lower Beth first.

"I know you're scared, Beth, but it will be fine, I promise you," Lorelei lied as convincingly as she could.

She knew the fire terrified her daughter, and she felt that way herself, but there was no way she would let Beth realize it. She slid up the window, feeling the draft pulling the smoke towards them. Then, she kicked out the screen sending it crashing to the sidewalk. She heard sirens approaching and leaned out, relieved when she saw flashing lights heading their way. Beth, to her credit, climbed out of the window with no hesitation whatsoever.

Atta girl! Lorelei thought.

She watched her daughter crawl backward over the small overhang with the sheet wrapped around her waist, and then she shimmied her way out of sight.

Dear God, please let her be okay, Lorelei prayed as she allowed the sheets to slide between her hands as gradually as she could. The material wasn't that long, but a police cruiser had screeched to a halt under the window, and she saw Artie, the deputy sheriff, jump up on its hood. Once Beth was safely in his arms, she let go of the sheet. She knew she should climb out of the window, and yet she didn't do that. Her brain was screaming that what she was about to do was not the smartest thing in the world, but Beth had been through enough.

She turned from the window, ran to the kitchen cupboard, pulled out a garbage bag, and stuffed one of the sofa cushions into it. Her laptop followed, then the keepsakes box and her purse. She dragged the sack into Beth's room and grabbed her daughter's favorite stuffed toys, her small collection of journals and her tablet, and shoved them into the bag hurriedly. She tied up the bag, ran to the window, and threw it as far as she could, praying that the cushion would protect it from the impact.

The fire broke through the front and bedroom doors at the same time she heard fire trucks arrive outside. With one final glance behind her, she ran to the window and climbed out, almost directly into the arms of a firefighter. He helped her to the ladder, and she climbed down and headed toward a nearby ambulance where Beth was wearing an oxygen mask.

Beth was safe, Lorelei thought, blinking back tears of joy, and nothing else mattered more than that.

Jefferson was about to pull out of his driveway, heading to pick up his sister when he saw Coop driving like a demon in the opposite direction. His brother never drove that fast unless it was life or death, and Jefferson went cold. Lorelei was in trouble. He didn't know how he knew that; he just did.

He turned his SUV around and followed his brother up Main Street, but it wasn't long before he had to pull over because the road had been closed off ahead. He could see emergency vehicles clustered between Toby's and the other side of the street. But, it was hard to focus on them when he could see flames shooting twenty feet into the air from the roof of his building, the building where Lorelei and Beth lived. The fire had consumed the whole second floor, and the rental apartments were burned almost to the studs. He watched firefighters spraying down the adjoining buildings to stop the fire from spreading.

His hands shook as he got out of the Explorer. He wanted to run the remaining few hundred feet, but he couldn't get his legs to work. Abject fear clogged his brain. I should have gone home with her, he thought. I should have just insisted they forget about picking up their things. He shouldered his way through the throng of people who'd taken to the streets to watch the firefighters at work, but he couldn't see much.

There were two ambulances ahead. Jefferson could see one of them, and it was empty apart from a paramedic. The other was parked in Toby's lot, but the doors were open, blocking him from getting a clear view. He couldn't see Coop anywhere, but he knew he was there somewhere.

"Jefferson!" He heard his name shouted out of nowhere and then spotted Toby barreling towards him. He couldn't remember seeing the diner owner ever move that fast. "They got out, they both got out in time. They're safe." All the breath rushed out of his body, and he felt light-headed. He didn't realize he'd staggered a little until Toby grabbed his arm to steady him. "I got you, boy, I got you!"

Thanking Toby, he made his way carefully through the chaos to the parking lot and around the back of the ambulance. Beth was sitting on the tailgate with an oxygen mask on, and Lorelei had her back to him, but when Beth smiled, Lorelei turned around. She looked exhausted, and she had sooty smudges on her face, but he'd never seen a woman look more beautiful.

She walked toward him, wrapped in a blanket that engulfed her tiny frame. He had a flashback to the moment he'd first seen her trudging with Beth in the bitter cold. He covered the yards separating them in a few long strides and wrapped his arms around her, burying his face in her hair. She smelled like shampoo mixed with smoke, and it hit him she could have died tonight, and she would never have known how he felt about her.

He pushed back from her, taking her face between his hands gently, tears filling his eyes. "This might not be the most romantic time to say this, but I love you, Lorelei, with all my heart and soul. I couldn't go another minute without telling you that."

She hiccupped, almost giggled, and then she threw her arms around his waist. As she broke down into gut-wrenching sobs, she clung to him as if her life depended on it, and all he could do was hold onto her. He didn't even mind that she hadn't said the words back to him. All he cared about was that she was alive. He picked her up and cradled her to his chest as he sat next to Beth on the tailgate of the ambulance. "You guys just took ten years off my life," he said to the little girl as she leaned against him.

Beth took off her oxygen mask long enough to whisper quietly, "I'm sorry." She smiled up at him, and his heart did that little flip it had done earlier when she'd hugged him. Oh yeah, his Dad was right; when it happened, love hit you like a freight train, and he loved this child with all his heart.

TEN

Lorelei felt so safe snuggled in Jefferson's protective embrace with Beth's head resting on her lap. They had been on the verge of disaster tonight, but they'd made it through, and that was all she could focus on. Then she heard voices yelling, but it was hard to make out what they were saying. When the paramedics from the other ambulance rushed by, she stood up, her legs shaking, terrified all over again.

Jefferson got to his feet too. "Stay here with Beth." His voice was gruffer than usual, a sure sign the paramedics' behavior had scared him too.

Lorelei watched as he sprinted over to the sheriff. Although she couldn't tell what they were saying from so far away, their body language spoke volumes. The fire had hurt someone they loved; she was sure. Please, don't let it be Jackson. Lorelei prayed fervently, but as Jefferson walked back toward the ambulance, she knew her prayer was in vain this time.

"Is he badly hurt?" Please let him be okay, she begged.

Jefferson shrugged, keeping his emotions reined in. "He must have gone back to the office for something. They found him out the back, in the stairwell, unconscious."

Beth whimpered and buried her face in her mother's lap. Lorelei hugged her, murmuring reassuringly. "Go to your brother Jefferson, he needs you."

He nodded, wrapping his arms around them briefly, and then ran over to the other ambulance.

"Is Jackson going to die?" Beth asked solemnly.

"I hope not," Lorelei answered honestly. "Just keep praying for him, it's the only thing we can do right now."

The paramedics returned and ushered them inside the ambulance for transportation to the emergency room. Lorelei knew she would feel better once the doctors thoroughly checked out Beth. Still, her daughter's breathing was already much improved. While they were at the hospital, they could find out how Jackson had faired too, but it seemed like time was traveling in reverse as the short journey seemed to take forever.

Jefferson traveled to the hospital with Jackson in the ambulance. The paramedics said his brother's vitals looked good, and although he was unconscious, he seemed to breathe regularly enough. Smoke inhalation was a silent killer, though. Jefferson was fully aware the fire could have far-reaching health implications for his twin. They would have to be patient and wait for the hospital to say Jackson was going to make a full recovery.

"Hang in there, Jack," he whispered in his brother's ear before they wheeled him through the doors to the examining area. Jefferson made his way to the front desk and filled out the paperwork, but his head was spinning. People he loved could have died tonight, was all he could focus on, and it made him feel sick to his stomach.

"Jefferson!" Grace hurtled through the main doors and threw herself into his arms, her whole body shaking. "Where is he? Did he get badly hurt? What happened? How are Lorelei and Beth?"

"Slow down, Gracie," he attempted a smile, but it didn't make it to his eyes. "As soon as I do this paperwork, we can all go back there and wait for news together, and you can see him."

"You're done, Mr. Cooper," the desk clerk said, holding out his insurance card and identification. "I'll buzz you back there now."

Jefferson was about to say they needed to wait for his father. Then Harry Cooper strode into the building, looking older than his almost sixty years for the first time. "We're ready to go now," Jefferson said, although he felt far from ready emotionally. This wasn't just his brother, it was his other half, the man he'd shared his mother's womb with, and it was his best friend.

"Your daughter will be fine," the doctor reassured Lorelei, and she breathed a sigh of relief. Still, the feeling was short-lived because Jackson was in the emergency room too. It had been several hours since they'd arrived, but she only knew they had found him unconscious, nothing more. How he had gotten that way was unknown, but she suspected he might have been overcome by smoke.

"Do you want a chocolate bar from the vending machine?" she asked.

"Thanks, Mom, I *am* hungry!"

Lorelei smiled as she pulled the curtain aside and then closed it again. Luckily, the whole experience with the fire had exhausted Beth, or she might have wondered how her mother could buy anything from a vending machine. Beth hadn't realized yet that they only had the clothes on their backs and nothing else.

Lorelei hadn't realized there were so many treatment rooms. But, most of them had the curtains open and no occupants. It wouldn't be too hard to find the Coopers, surely? She thought.

"Lorelei!" Harry Cooper hurried around the corner, right in front of her. He wrapped his arms around her, and she felt like crying all over again. This man, whose son was being treated somewhere in the hospital, was comforting her when she thought she should be doing that for him.

She pulled back, studying Jefferson's father. "How is Jackson?" She held her breath, praying harder than she ever had before. God had been on her side once today, and she hoped He still was.

"Jackson's going to be fine. He left his wallet in his desk at the office and went back for it. He said the fire was already blazing on the floor above as he went to leave," Harry explained.

She felt tears trickling down her cheeks as she bit her bottom lip hard. Jackson was awake and talking, the miracles kept right on coming.

"I think maybe you should sit down," Harry said.

"No, I'm fine, just relieved," Lorelei began. Something about Harry's expression gave her pause as he ushered her toward one of the standard-issue plastic hospital chairs in the corridor. "What is it, Harry? What aren't you telling me?"

Jefferson's father rubbed his chin with one hand as he reached out his other hand and wrapped it around her shoulders. "Jackson was unconscious because a piece of pipe hit him." He paused for Lorelei to take that in. "The pipe didn't fall on his head. Someone picked it up and hit him with it from behind. The security camera out back of the office was still recording to the cloud at that point. It showed a man running out and getting into a vehicle driven by a woman."

"Why would anyone do that to him? Was it a robbery gone wrong?" Lorelei was so tired she could barely even process the information.

Jackson was awake and talking. He had a concussion and was staying at the hospital overnight for observation. The doctor was sure there was no cause for concern, but that didn't reassure Jefferson much. It was his twin they were talking about, and he'd never realized how deeply he loved his brother until this moment.

Grace was sitting beside Jackson chatting to him, and their Dad had gone for some coffee. "I'm just going to see how Beth is," he said, not entirely lying because he did want to check on her.

Jackson smiled and reached out, and they clasped hands before Jefferson pulled the curtain and headed for the nurses' station to ask where Beth was. He barely made it around the corner when he saw his father at the far end of the corridor with his arm around Lorelei's shoulder. Was she crying? His heart froze in his chest. Dear God, please don't let it be Beth.

"Hey Jefferson, have you seen Dad?" Coop's voice came from behind him, and Jefferson turned around. "Whoa dude, you look like you're about to pass out."

Jefferson nodded his head toward Lorelei. "She's crying."

"He probably told her," Coop replied cryptically.

"It's not about Beth?"

"No, she's fine, I took her chocolate milk and a banana, the poor kid is exhausted, but hungry," Coop said. "Take a deep breath, Jeff, because this may be difficult to hear."

Jefferson didn't want to take a breath, he wanted to know what the hell was going on that caused his usually calm brother to look like he wanted to kick someone's ass. "Just tell me already."

"We're ninety-nine percent sure it was Malcolm who hit Jack over the head with the pipe, and he likely started the fire too. I showed Daniel a still from the video footage of a man entering the building, he had no doubt it was Lorelei's husband," Coop said. "The fire chief found a lot of accelerant in the hall outside the apartments, and the smoke detectors on that level were deliberately disabled. The middle apartment was probably where the fire started because it went up really fast. The security camera caught him as he left and got into a car with a woman driving," Coop finished.

Jefferson released his breath slowly. Whatever he had been expecting from his brother, it sure as hell hadn't been that. There was no doubt in his mind that Lorelei's husband had set the fire. Was he trying to kill her or just make her suffer for leaving him? Was the fire payback or something worse? Either way, he realized it didn't matter. He clapped his brother on the shoulder and set off at a jog down the long corridor. Nothing else mattered but getting to Lorelei.

His Dad saw him first and stood up, leaving Lorelei hunched over on her chair. She had her arms wrapped tightly around herself as if she were trying to hold herself together. She looked up as he sat down next to her. "I'm so sorry, Jefferson, it's all my fault," she sobbed.

"Are you kidding me?" That she was blaming herself made him want to punch a hole in the hospital's drywall. He realized Lorelei was staring at him, through glistening lashes, her blue eyes brimming with tears. "None of this is your fault. That bastard, Malcolm, could have killed you and Beth, and even if he didn't know you were home, he sure as hell whacked my brother over the head, that part was no accident."

Lorelei's eyes widened in shock, and Jefferson realized her conversation with his Dad hadn't reached that point yet. "I may have gotten ahead of myself. Jackson is fine, he has a concussion, but he'll recover. Someone hit him over the head with a piece of pipe. They're checking it for prints, but the security camera footage is hard to doubt. Malcolm was there. Daniel identified him."

"Why would he do something like this?" she asked in a small voice.

Jefferson looked to his Dad, the former sheriff, because he, as sure as heck, didn't have the answer. Harry shrugged. "I think maybe he was looking for something he thought you had and perhaps set the building on fire to cover his tracks. Did you take anything of his when you left him?"

Lorelei shook her head, and Jefferson couldn't imagine why she would have wanted to take any reminders of the man with her. "Let's leave this alone for tonight. Is Beth allowed to go home?" She nodded, and he stood, pulling her with him and wrapping his arms around her tightly. "Let's go get *our* little girl." He chose his words deliberately, waiting to see how she would respond to his claim of ownership. Her eyes brimmed again, and she hugged him so tightly he knew he hadn't crossed a line. He caught his Dad's eye and saw he wasn't unaffected by the words either. Harry Cooper simply nodded in response, but his meaning was clear.

When they walked around the corner to Beth's cubicle, an officer was sitting on a chair outside. Lorelei stuttered to a halt before looking up at him sadly. "I can't believe I brought this man into our lives."

"He wasn't like this then, I'm sure," Jefferson reassured her.

"No, he wasn't. He was charming and romantic, and attentive. I know it was all an act now, but he was great at playing that role, at least until after the lawyer married us," she said sadly.

"Let's get Beth and go home." She looked askance at him, and he dropped a gentle kiss on her nose. "You live with me now, no strings, no pressure. We'll be roomies until you're ready for more. I have plenty of space."

"We can stay at your house?" Beth's head poked around the curtain. She looked pale but alert, and she was smiling. "Do you have a big TV?"

Jefferson snorted out a laugh. "I have a decent-sized television and game systems and a computer, and two extra bedrooms. There's one for you and one for your Mom."

"I have my tablet and some stuff that Mom threw out of a window before she climbed out. The deputy told me the bag landed on a bush," Beth was grinning then, and Lorelei laughed as she hugged her.

"You stuck around long enough in a burning building to grab some of Beth's things?" Jefferson wasn't sure if he wanted to yell at her for being so reckless or kiss her.

"I know, it was stupid, several people have pointed that out already, including your big brother," Lorelei looked chagrined.

"You are an amazing woman, but next time, leave the stuff. Beth can live without her iPad, but neither one of us can live without *you*!" He smiled, and she reached up a hand and placed it on his cheek gently. He couldn't resist dropping a kiss on her lips, forgetting they had an audience. The officer sitting on the chair pretended a wall poster on resuscitation fascinated him. But, Beth was staring right at them, grinning like the Cheshire Cat. "I love your Mom," he told her. Why bother pretending?

Beth nodded. "I know. She loves you too."

"*Beth*!" Lorelei shot her daughter a wide-eyed look and then blushed fiercely.

Jefferson laughed out loud. "Let's get you discharged, young lady. Before you reveal all of your Mom's secrets to me!"

Lorelei stepped inside Jefferson's house for the first time and smiled. She'd only previously seen it from the driveway, which seemed so long ago after all that had happened recently. She walked through the front door. This was Jefferson's home, and she loved how the family room flowed into the kitchen and dining area, creating a wide-open space. The furniture was modern and homey.

Even the gray color on the walls was welcoming, and the couch looked so good she wanted to curl up on it and go right to sleep. She couldn't, though, she knew, because she needed to settle Beth into bed first.

"You look like you're about to fall asleep standing up," Grace whispered to her. Lorelei agreed. Her attention was drawn to Beth, who was already nodding in Jefferson's arms.

Lorelei couldn't help thinking how fragile her daughter looked and how lucky they had been today. Not knowing if Malcolm knew they were home, or not, was the worst part about the whole ordeal. If he had known, then the deputy sitting in his patrol car off the side of the driveway, was a welcome addition to Jefferson's front yard. But if Malcolm *had* known, she thought anxiously, then the man was a sociopath, and that was genuinely terrifying. For once, she hoped Malcolm wasn't quite as evil as he seemed!

"Follow me, Grace has set up the spare bedrooms for you," Jefferson strode down a hall off the kitchen, and she trotted to keep up.

When she walked into the first bedroom, she saw Beth's soft toys lined up beside the bed and her tablet on the nightstand charging up. Then she spotted a bag on the floor and looked at Grace, who smiled. "There's a twenty-four-hour Walmart close to here. I got a few basic items to see her through the next couple of days."

Lorelei nodded, biting her lip as she watched Jefferson place her now sleeping daughter on the bed, covering her with blankets. "Thank you."

"There's a bathroom between this room and the other guest room. I put toothbrushes and a few other things in there," Grace ushered her out of one bedroom and down the hall to another, where she found a second plastic bag.

It was no use; she couldn't hold back her emotions any longer. Tears flowed unchecked until Grace and Jefferson engulfed her in a group hug, and she clung to them like a drowning woman who'd found a life vest.

She could cry so silently, Jefferson marveled, always concerned for her daughter Beth, and clearly not wanting her to awaken to sobbing. "I think I need to wash my face and brush my teeth," she took a deep, calming breath, and they watched as she made her way to the guest bathroom.

"Are you sure you can't stay over?" he asked his sister, feeling ill-equipped to deal with the raw emotion coming off Lorelei in waves right now.

"I want to get home to Dad. This thing with Jackson shook him to his core. You've got this, Jeff. You love her, she loves you. Just be there for her, it's all she really needs," Grace hugged him tightly, her eyes betraying how exhausted she felt.

They headed back to the kitchen when headlights flashed across the living room as someone pulled up outside. Jefferson walked to the front window, just to be sure the car belonged to Coop. "Looks like your ride home is here."

Grace called her goodbyes to Lorelei before heading out to Coop's SUV. "Text me when you get home," he told her, and his brother shot him a thumbs up. Artie waved from his cruiser, and Jefferson wanted to invite him to come in, out of the cold, but he knew better. They had a guard for a reason, and someone would relieve Artie in a few hours. Coop had instructed Jefferson to arm his security system and be on alert. This was so not how he'd thought this week might end.

He closed the front door and armed the security panel, kicking off his boots before making his way into the kitchen. He wondered if he had any leftovers in the fridge because he'd just discovered he was starving. The microwave was beeping as Lorelei walked into the kitchen several minutes later. She'd brushed her hair and washed off the sooty smudges he'd been getting used to seeing on her cheeks, and she looked so tired.

He took the pasta out and held up the bowl. "Want to share?"

She smiled, and he could see her inhaling the delicious cheesy scent. "Your sister is a fantastic cook. I could definitely eat."

He knew he looked smug. "You're looking at the chef right here. I can cook a few of my Mom's recipes, and this is one of my personal favorites." He divided the concoction into two bowls and walked over to the dining table. "There are glasses in that cupboard behind you and silverware in the drawer beneath."

"What would you like?" she asked, and the intimacy of the question struck him.

"You," he grinned boyishly at her. "But, I'll settle for some milk."

He watched as she grabbed glasses and carried them over to the fridge, and then filled them. She brought them to the table and then got two spoons before she sat down across from him. "You could sit next to me, I don't bite."

She shook her head. "I like being able to look at you, it makes me feel safe." She reached across the table to take his hand in hers, and he felt that familiar jolt of awareness.

He understood where she was coming from. He didn't want to let her out of his sight for a moment, either. He was even feeling antsy about Beth being so far down the hall. His phone pinged, breaking the moment, and he looked down to see a text message from his sister.

"Grace made it home?"

He nodded.

"She bought me underwear and some jeans, and a tee-shirt and she got Beth two outfits and even a nightshirt. She's always so thoughtful," Lorelei said.

Jefferson smiled. "She's been that way her whole life. Her birth mother gave her the perfect name, she is always gracious."

"I can't believe her mother abandoned her in the back of your Dad's police car," Lorelei said softly.

"It was his own car actually. She had a piece of paper pinned to the baby blanket wrapping her that said, *take care of Grace,*" he almost felt like he could remember that day. But, he'd only been six years old, so his memory was more an amalgamation of everyone else's stories.

"And they never figured out who left her there?"

He shook his head sadly. "We even got her one of those DNA kits last year for Christmas, and she put herself into a database, but so far no hits. I think Grace has accepted that she might never know."

They were sitting on the couch an hour later watching HGTV when Lorelei realized she could hear soft snoring. Jefferson had slouched at one end of the sofa, his feet resting on the coffee table. She'd burrowed into a pile of cushions at the other end with her toes just about touching his thigh. His expression was solemn even when he was asleep, she thought, like a man who was always in control. But one errant strand of hair had fallen across his forehead, and she couldn't resist scooching down to the other end of the sofa to tuck it back into place.

He woke as soon as her fingers brushed his temple, and his fierce expression startled her, then he smiled sleepily. "Some bodyguard I am, huh?"

She shook her head and slipped into the crook of his arm, snuggling into his warmth. "You make me feel safer than I ever have, even though I know Malcolm is out there somewhere. Have I ever told you how glad I am that we hit that deer?"

He laughed, and she felt the vibration throughout her body. She looked up at him and found his gaze locked with hers. She had thought she was beyond tired when they'd arrived at his house, but now she was totally wired. There was only one thing she wanted right now: him. She shifted, so she was sitting across his lap, all the while maintaining eye contact. She needed to touch him so badly, and judging by his expression, he felt the same. She moved closer and felt his body tense.

They had promised to wait, but after today's events, why should they? She rolled off his lap, got to her feet, and watched him try to hold his disappointment in check. It disappeared when she straddled his lap and brought her face a breath away from his. His eyes widened as she pressed her entire body hard up against him and slid her arms around his neck. She kissed him slowly, moving her whole body against his as she changed position, and he groaned. She pulled back with a mischievous expression in her eyes. "I was hoping this was a participation sport," she quipped.

His hands were on her instantly, curving around her back, sliding under her smoky, soot smudged shirt, his thumbs finding their way under the edge of her bra. Oh yes, she thought, this was just what she needed.

I'm going to explode, Jefferson thought. The woman he loved was grinding herself into him, and she wasn't about to stop his hands from continuing their journey to those luscious breasts of hers. He wanted to get up and carry her to his bed. But, he was sure any movement right now would see him embarrassing himself like a horny teenager.

His mouth found hers and their tongues tangled, jabbing, and twisting together in their impatience, then he felt her hands on his belt and froze. "Lorelei…?"

"I want you, Jefferson, I want you so much," her voice was husky, her eyelids drooping sexily.

I can't believe I'm about to do this, he thought, but he couldn't take advantage of her today, no matter how much he wanted her. "Lorelei, we need to stop."

"What?" She sounded groggy.

"I can't do this, you've been through too much today, you're not thinking straight."

"*What*?" She didn't sound groggy now. "You don't want to make love?"

"Oh, I want to, I think you should be able to feel that," he joked.

He realized too late she didn't find his joke particularly amusing. She looked pissed, then her chin lifted defiantly, and she smiled sweetly. Oh, I'm in trouble now, he thought, watching as she pushed herself back far enough to put some distance between their bodies. He'd thought she was about to get up, but then she tugged on the hem of her shirt and pulled it up over her head in one fluid movement.

"Lorelei, what are you trying to do to me?"

She raised her eyebrows. "I would have thought that was obvious," she said as she reached behind her.

Hell no, he thought, if this was happening, the bra was his domain.

Lorelei felt his hands on hers as she reached behind her for the clasp of her bra and heard him growl territorially. *"Mine."*

She looked into his eyes and knew she'd finally pushed him far enough that his chivalry would no longer hold him in check. As soon as he unhooked her bra, she felt liberated. She arched away from him, baring herself to his hungry gaze. She felt him reach between her legs, his fingers seeking out her feminine core and almost jackknifed off him. He was expertly rubbing her through her leggings, and she was so ready for him; it was almost unbearable.

He slid his hands under her butt and stood in one fluid motion. She wasn't sure where he was going until he laid her gently onto the sofa. She felt him slide his fingers into the waistband of her leggings, and then he pulled them down until he reached the hem of her boring cotton panties. He hooked those too and slid them both down to her ankles, then he was on top of her, and she couldn't resist reaching for his belt and unbuckling him.

"This is probably not going to be epic," he said solemnly, and she reached up to touch his cheek gently before returning to her task, freeing him from his jeans. She didn't push his pants down, she kicked off her leggings, so she could wrap her legs around his waist, pushing herself hard against the length of him. She was so wet and ready for him that his first thrust had her muscles clenching around him. His mouth found one nipple then the other. His lips caressed her neck and then trailed up to her mouth. Then he went still, and she knew it was because he was trying so hard to make their first time special.

He pushed her down into the pile of cushions, and she felt him withdraw from her and was instantly bereft, but then his lips trailed down across her breasts, then her stomach, heading south. His tongue teased her gently, finding its way to that little nub of pleasure she had been grinding up against him earlier. Oh wow, he knew what he was doing, she thought, as he flicked and circled and nibbled and sucked on her.

He briefly made eye contact and then started a rhythmic, gentle sucking that had her reaching for a pillow to cover her face to muffle her cries. She couldn't control the wild bucking of her hips as he brought her to the pinnacle. She threw the pillow aside and grasped him by his hair, pulling him north. She saw him then, in all his glory, and his arousal was magnificent.

"I need you inside me right now, don't make me wait!" she begged.

He complied with one fluid upward surge and pushed her down into the sofa cushions. She'd thought she wanted to curl up on this couch earlier, but this was much better. Their lips tangled erotically. His hands were all over her. Their bodies were coming together as he thrust into her again and again. She felt him tense, and she snaked her legs around him, slamming her hips into his, grinding her softness into his opposing hardness. She felt herself coming again, and somewhere in the middle of her release, she felt him tense before he collapsed on top of her.

What the hell had just happened? Jefferson thought as he righted his clothes, zipping his pants. She'd seduced him like a vixen, and he'd loved every minute, but he hoped she wouldn't regret it when she awoke in the morning.

"Time for bed," he announced, draping a throw around her as he picked her up from the couch and headed for the guest room where he deposited her on the bed. "I'll be back with your clothes."

"Okay," she whispered sleepily.

He was still dressed, his body now in a semi-aroused state, and he felt like he'd taken advantage of her, but he couldn't make himself feel sorry. He stopped by his bedroom on the way back from the living room and grabbed a tee-shirt from his dresser, but when he got back to the guest room, he found her curled up on top of the quilt, naked and sound asleep.

He dropped a kiss on her shoulder and draped the tee shirt over her sleeping form before pulling the quilt over her. He wanted to stay and wake up with her in his arms. But he knew, tonight had been a moment out of time. In the morning, later in the morning, since it was after two already, they would continue as they had been, waiting for her divorce decree. Only then would they make their relationship official. Until that time, he was sure tonight's amorous adventure would hold him for the foreseeable future.

ELEVEN

Lorelei awoke to sun filtering hazily through the bedroom curtains. The clock on the wall said it was only seven, and she stretched languorously like a sleepy feline. The quilt slipped down, the material rasping against nipples that felt more than a little tender. With a start, she realized she was naked.

Oh, my God! Last night, the fire, the hospital, and then that hot, sensual, amazing coupling with Jefferson on the couch. In the cold light of day, her behavior seemed insanely inappropriate. What on earth was she going to say to him? How was she even going to face him? She sat up and realized there was a tee-shirt under the quilt with her, and she put it on, smiling when it reached to mid-thigh. Even after what had happened, Jefferson had still been thoughtful enough to leave her something to wear, he was a special man.

She realized she needed to check on Beth before she got dressed, so she padded down the hall, only to find the door wide open and the bed empty.

"Hi Mom, you slept until lunchtime!" Beth's voice called out.

Lorelei looked down the hall and saw Beth was on the couch playing a video game on Jefferson's television.

"What time is it?"

"Almost noon," Jefferson answered from behind her, and she started guiltily.

"That's not what the clock in my room says."

Jefferson laughed. "Yeah, never reset it after the power went out a few weeks ago. Sorry. I thought you needed to sleep in, Beth thought so too."

She was suddenly aware she was only wearing a tee-shirt, *his shirt.* "It looks good on you," he said huskily, reading her mind.

She blushed, and she didn't know where to look, so she found a spot in the middle of his chest to focus on. "Last night was… it was just…"

He took a quick look down the hall and then hustled her back into the guest room and closed the door behind them. "Last night was amazing, incredible, the best night of my life," he said, backing her up against the door.

She gulped. That tingling feeling had started up again as Jefferson pressed himself against her. He ran a finger down from her neck across the first breast's burgeoning peak and then the other. Her nipples puckered; their outline clear through his old college shirt. He slid his arms around her waist and down to cup her butt, and then he groaned. "You're killing me, Lorelei."

"Oh!" She tried to pull away, realizing he'd discovered she wasn't wearing any underwear. It was déjà vu all over again.

"I'd love to follow you up those stairs now," he murmured, nuzzling her neck as he slid his hands under *his* shirt. Her skin was so silky, and he loved how it felt. He watched as she blushed again, amazed she could still do that after what they'd shared the night before.

They couldn't do anything about the instant chemistry they had between them, not with Beth awake nearby, so he backed off. "I cleaned up in the family room this morning, and I must have been loud enough to wake Beth. I made scrambled eggs for her. There was no evidence of anything happening between us." He carefully chose his words, but her deepening blush let him know she understood what he was referring to.

"You have a really nice home," she mumbled, changing the subject abruptly.

What was going through her head now? He wondered. Unless…

"I chose this house because of the land it had around it. I figured I'd get a dog for the company one day, but it's been two years already," he observed her reaction, and sure enough, there was her tell, that little hitch in her breath right when he'd said two years. Even though he was trying hard to keep his hands off her, he couldn't resist gathering her against his chest. "She was never here, Lorelei, this has only ever been my home. She would have hated it, it's not chic enough. It doesn't even have much curb appeal."

"I suppose I'll never get to look at that photo she sent you now," she laughed up into his face, and he faked a scowl. "Unless the phone survived the fire."

"If it did, I'll burn it myself," he growled, pressing a gentle kiss on her upturned lips. "Now I'm going back to get my butt whipped by your daughter at Mario Kart. Then, we can go shopping, so you can stop going commando around me because it's killing me, knowing there's only a tee shirt between us."

"Is there any news?" she whispered as he reached for the door handle.

He shook his head. "Coop promised he'd call if they found out anything. My Dad also called Danny to let him know where you were at, I hope you don't mind?"

She shook her head, and he let himself out and went back to join Beth, who paused her video game as he sat down next to her. "You and my Mom closed the door to the bedroom."

"Um, yeah, we did," Jefferson's mind was scrambling for a plausible explanation.

"Were you talking about Malcolm?"

"Yes," he said, which wasn't flat out lying to the girl. "But we don't have any news yet. We were also talking about how we need to go shopping because neither one of you has many clothes."

Beth grinned and then wrinkled her nose. "Do you think there are any thrift stores around here we could go to?"

"Sure," Jefferson replied before he caught on. "Are you worried about how to pay for everything?" Beth nodded glumly. "Don't be. I have a surprise for you both. People have been dropping off gift cards at the diner. Toby said they have about thirty from diner patrons and locals who heard about the fire. You guys have made quite the impression!"

Beth squealed and jumped into his arms, kneeing him in the stomach hard enough to have him sucking in his breath painfully. A little lower, he thought, and Lorelei would have nothing to worry about for a few days!

"What's all the commotion?" Lorelei said, walking into the room, wearing his college shirt and the jeans Grace had bought for her, but he was sure she was wearing a bra this time.

Beth scrambled off the couch and ran to her. "People at the diner have donated gift cards so we can get clothes because they like you so much!"

Lorelei looked askance at him, and Jefferson nodded. "She's right - regulars have been coming in all morning, Toby told me when he called."

"Can we eat at the diner and then go shopping?" Beth asked.

"Sure," Jefferson and Lorelei answered in unison.

"I'll get ready now!"

Lorelei walked into the kitchen. "Can I make a coffee?"

"You don't need to ask, Lorelei, you live here, remember?"

She blushed again, and he realized he liked making her do that. "You're still wearing my shirt."

"Had to," she said, without explanation.

"Because…?"

She lifted the over-sized shirt up and pirouetted. Holy crap! It looked as if someone painted the jeans straight onto her body. "Yeah, we need to get you some jeans in the right size," he laughed as she dropped the shirt again. "Although I have to say, I'm a pretty big fan of this pair."

"Stop teasing me like that, or everyone will know what we've been up to."

He hated to disillusion her, but he was pretty sure Coop had guessed when he'd dropped by earlier to give him an update, but he kept that little fact to himself.

Bags and bags of clothes littered Jefferson's family room as Beth showed off her booty to Grace and Madison. Lorelei sat at the dining table with the rest of the Cooper clan and Danny and Toby. "How could they just disappear?" she asked. Surely someone must have seen the car.

"The plates on it were stolen," Coop shrugged. "They picked one of the most common makes and models, so there's no way to run all of those registrations down. Don't worry, I'm sure we will catch a break at some point when they make a mistake."

She nodded, knowing he was right, but it was so frustrating. Jefferson reached across the table and squeezed her hand, and she felt like she could breathe again. She caught Danny's eye before he looked pointedly at Jefferson, and it was clear he knew something had changed. She watched as the two men made eye contact until Danny gave a small nod. God, men, were so territorial, she thought.

"I'd better get Madison home," Danny stood then, reaching out to shake Jefferson's hand.

"Oh, Dad!" Madison protested.

"Can't she stay over, please?" Beth asked. "They're coming to lunch tomorrow, anyway."

Lorelei was about to explain why this wasn't possible when Jefferson cut in. "If it's okay with your Dad, it's okay with me. We have plenty of extra clothes," he laughed at the piles draped all over the sofa.

"I can pick you up from Harry's tomorrow," Danny walked over to give his daughter a hug, and then looked at Jefferson. "If you're sure?"

Lorelei watched as Grace shuffled out of Danny's way, looking uncomfortable, probably because she hadn't had time to apologize for jumping all over him about Malcolm the day before.

Suddenly everyone was getting ready to leave and head home or over to the hospital to visit Jackson. He was being discharged in the morning. He had a lump on the back of his head, some stitches, and some minor burns, but he'd been lucky because the lower level hadn't caught fire the same as the upper. Even their legal files had survived in their fireproof cabinets. Still, most everything else had suffered scorching or smoke and water damage.

It was so quiet after everyone left, apart from the giggling of two little girls, and Lorelei closed her eyes to drink in the sound. She felt the heat of him as he walked up behind her, and then he slid his arms around her and nuzzled her neck. "Thank you for letting her stay over."

Jefferson snorted. "Like I didn't have an ulterior motive. An occupied Beth means I can enjoy a fashion show while you try on all those new clothes."

"I tried them on in the store," Lorelei pointed out.

"Spoilsport!"

"I'm keeping this shirt," she whispered as she turned around to face him, his arms still hooked around her waist.

"Nope, my shirt, I'm taking it back later," his eyes went dark, and she shivered in anticipation, but made no move to argue.

After two pizzas and several rounds of team Mario Kart, Jefferson realized why most parents looked equal parts tired and frustrated. Sitting next to Lorelei as they battled the two girls, losing miserably every time, he'd been hyper-aware of her thigh pressing against his. She was still wearing the disreputable jeans because she hadn't had the chance to change when everyone descended *en masse* to visit. Their snug fit was causing all kinds of inappropriate thoughts to fly through his brain.

"Can we watch some movies on Netflix?" Beth asked.

"It's getting late," Lorelei replied. "How about you get into your pajamas, and maybe we can let you have a slumber party out here?" The girls jumped up immediately and ran to the guest room.

"You are a genius," Jefferson murmured, sliding a hand up her thigh, heading for her waistband before she batted it away playfully.

"You tidy up the games, and I'll make them some snacks and drinks. Then I seem to remember you mentioning something about having a television in your room. Maybe we can watch something too?" She suggested.

"Can we at least fool around a little?" He raised an eyebrow, and she rewarded him with an endearing blush. "Right then, let's get this slumber party started."

It was only ten minutes into the action movie Lorelei had chosen when he saw her eyelids droop. She kept opening them widely, blinking hard, but to no avail, they would close again within seconds. He couldn't really blame her for being exhausted, it had been a hell of a day for her and her daughter. He slid out from under her and settled her against his pillows. Then he went to check on the two girls, who were far from asleep.

"Is Mom okay?" Beth asked.

"She fell asleep already," he said with a smile.

Beth and Madison giggled before Beth spoke again. "She stole your bed!"

Jefferson shrugged. "It's a king-size, there's still room for me, so long as I don't breathe. Now, don't stay up all night watching movies."

"We won't," the girls chorused, and he headed back to his room.

He undressed in the dark and slipped on a pair of pajama bottoms and climbed into bed beside Lorelei. She'd tied her hair up high on her head for practicality, but he couldn't resist taking it down. Slowly, so as not to wake her, he slid the hair tie off her curls and placed it on the bedside table. Her hair sprang free, riotously curly, and so soft. It smelled of something flowery; he wasn't sure what it was, but he wanted to bury his face in it and stay there all night.

She moved in her sleep and moaned. It was a bad dream, Jefferson realized. He stroked her hair and murmured reassuring words in her ear until she calmed again. He wanted her so much he could barely contain it, but what she needed tonight was a protector. Someone to watch over her. Someone who would make sure no one would ever harm her again. No man would take that job away from him, Jefferson vowed, she was his. He pulled her closer, spooning against her back, sliding his arm around her waist, and within seconds he was asleep too.

Lorelei woke slowly, confused by the weight pinning her waist until she saw that it belonged to an arm, a very muscular, male arm. It had been a long time since she'd woken in a man's embrace. Malcolm had not been one to snuggle, and Beth's Dad had died so long ago she could barely remember what it felt like to be held by him. She wanted to stay there, wrapped in Jefferson's arms. But, she needed a glass of water and to check on Beth and Madison too.

She slid out from under him, and his hand grazed her breast, making her aware of how closely they had slept all night. She wanted to climb back into the bed, and seduce him awake, but they'd made a deal. They could fool around some, but she wanted to be a free woman before giving herself to him again. But, oh Lord, just watching him sprawled out, shirtless, sleeping, was making her so hot she could barely keep her hands off him.

A quick glance at the clock told her it was only six a.m. She padded quietly into the kitchen, swinging by the couch on her way to check on the sleeping girls. They snuggled close together on the pull-out with the TV remote between them and looked like they could sleep for a while longer.

She filled a glass and was on her way back to the guest bedroom when Jefferson's door opened. Six feet of hellishly gorgeous male leaned on the doorjamb, his pajama bottoms riding dangerously low on his hips. "You're up early."

"Thirsty," she croaked out as her mouth went dry at the sight of him.

Jefferson raised an eyebrow. "See something you like?"

"I, um, that is, you're making this so hard, Jefferson," his smirk alerted her to her unfortunate choice of words. "Don't even say anything!"

"Take a shower with me, and I won't say another word."

"We definitely cannot do that!" she whispered fiercely. There was no way she could envisage being naked, under cascading water with soap bubbles and have that not end in hot, sweaty sex. "You're not playing fair; you know we made a deal, and you know how much I want you."

He hadn't been entirely sure the desire was mutual, until she spoke, despite Friday's late-night seduction. "I slept with my arms around you last night, and I behaved like a total gentleman. Are you suggesting if we showered together, you wouldn't be able to behave like a lady?" He couldn't resist teasing her a little more.

"Yes, that is exactly what I'm saying," she retorted primly.

Crap, major backfire, he thought. He had only been joking about the shower. But, Lorelei's eyes had turned that electric shade of blue. Now all he could think about was how very much he wanted to step under that spray with her and sponge down every delicious inch of her skin.

"Sorry Lorelei, I was only messing with you. I guess the joke's on me now."

"It is?" she looked confused as if she didn't know what to make of his teasing.

"Believe me, I'd love to shower with you. I was just trying to flirt with you. I'm sorry, I guess I'm more out of practice with women than I thought," he said.

She smiled then and stepped toward him, nudging him back into his bedroom. She pushed him across the room until the back of his knees hit the bed, and then she shoved hard, and he fell back on the mattress. She grabbed the hem of her shirt - his shirt - and slowly raised it over her head while he watched mesmerized from his reclining position, and then she threw it on the bed next to him.

She was wearing a tiny pair of panties and nothing else when she walked to the door and looked back over her shoulder. "You said you wanted your tee shirt back," she said, and then she sauntered across the hall to the main bathroom. He heard the lock click into place as the door closed behind her.

Lorelei leaned against the door panels, shocked at herself for behaving so brazenly. Then she heard a shout of laughter from Jefferson.

"Touché!" He called.

She glimpsed her face in the mirror as she set the shower running and waited for the water to get warm. She looked smug. She looked sexy, and happy too. She stepped into the bath and under the spray and let the water pound against her body. If he were in the shower with me, Lorelei thought, he would be inside me by now. Oh, how she wished he were.

Why did doing the right thing have to be so complicated? She'd never wanted a man more in her life, and she'd made a stupid pact to wait until she was a free woman. Then she'd broken that agreement two nights before, and now she knew what she was missing. What the hell had she been thinking? Jefferson only had to look at her with that twinkle in his eyes, and she wanted to tear his clothes off. Now she was staying in his home, sleeping only feet away from him, or like last night, pressed against him. How much longer could they possibly keep their hands off each other?

Jefferson stepped out of his shower and heard his cellphone ringing. It was Coop's ringtone, and as it was barely seven on a Sunday morning, he knew it had to be something important. "What's up?" He said, praying they'd caught Malcolm.

"Jeff, we have the woman," his brother said.

"You caught her?"

Coop cleared his throat on the other end of the line. "Not exactly. She walked into the office at around five this morning, confessed to who she was, and then said she wasn't doing any more talking until she speaks to Lorelei."

"What?" Jefferson couldn't contain his surprise.

"If Lorelei refuses, I'm sure the woman will talk to us. I figured you could run it by her, see how she feels about it?" Coop said.

Jefferson promised to talk to Lorelei as soon as they had a moment. But that didn't happen for a while because the girls were up, and she was cooking them breakfast. He found he liked watching her moving around his kitchen. It was as if she had always been there and as if she belonged there. She caught his eye a couple of times, and he could see she had picked up on his tension, but he wanted to wait until they were alone to broach the subject.

When the girls went to brush their teeth, Lorelei cornered him by the sink. "Spill it," she said impatiently. "What was that phone call about?"

He hadn't been sure she'd heard his phone ring earlier, but now he knew she had there seemed no point in beating about the bush. "Coop called to ask if you would go down to the office and talk to a suspect."

"Who is it?" Her voice trembled a little.

He didn't like seeing the fear that had crept into her eyes. "Not him," he reassured her. "The woman he was with turned herself in this morning, and she wants to talk to you. Coop said you don't have to, and he will be there the whole time, but it's up to you."

"Why does she want to talk to me?" Lorelei asked.

"She wouldn't say, but if you don't want to do this, then don't."

She looked scared and conflicted, and he reached out for her at the same moment she leaned into him.

She was safe, so long as she was in his arms, she thought. But what did this woman want with her? Why did she need to see her? Lorelei couldn't come up with any reason, other than maybe to apologize for what she'd been a part of. Was there really any need to talk to the woman just to make *her* feel better?

"I don't know what to do," she whispered into his chest as he held her.

"What is your gut telling you?" he said. "That's what my Dad judges everything by."

She took a deep breath and pulled back to look him in the eye. "It's saying I should see what she wants since I have nothing to lose."

"Then we have our answer, don't we?" he said.

She didn't want to disturb the girls as they sounded like they were playing in the guest room, and Artie was still sitting in the driveway on his second night of guard duty. Jefferson arranged for the deputy to drive her to the station while he stayed with Beth and Madison.

Lorelei wrote a quick note for her daughter, telling her she had to go make a statement at the sheriff's office, and then put on her coat. "Everything will be all right," Jefferson promised her as he handed her over to Artie.

Artie nodded and held the door on his cruiser open for her to get in the front, then he went around to the driver's door, and Lorelei heard Jefferson tell him to look after her. Her feeling of dread eased somewhat as she listened to his words, but every yard they drove closer to the sheriff's office, the knot in her stomach increased tenfold. When they pulled up, and Jefferson's brother was standing outside waiting for her, she wondered if she could go through with it. Then she heard Jefferson's voice inside her head again: *everything will be all right,* and she knew it would be.

TWELVE

The sheriff's office in Lake Thomas was small, with only one interrogation room and one cell because they didn't have enough crime to warrant a bigger space. The larger towns nearby had better facilities, but Lake Thomas was only busy over the summer months when campers, cabin owners, and festival-goers, came to town.

Lorelei perched on the edge of a chair in Sheriff Lucas Cooper's office, waiting to go into the interrogation room. The woman's name turned out to be Tania Wilton, and they would handcuff her to the table during their conversation. Nevertheless, Coop had assured her there was no reason to be afraid as he would be there.

"We're ready for you," he said, coming back into the room.

Here goes nothing, Lorelei thought. She walked through the main waiting area and across the hall and into the room where she saw the woman for the first time. Her hair wasn't quite the right shade of blond, and her curls looked more cultivated than natural, but the resemblance would have been close enough to match her ID for the bank teller.

"You must be Lorelei," the woman met her gaze a little unsteadily.

"I can see how you fooled everyone," Lorelei couldn't keep her distaste for the woman out of her voice.

"I'm sorry. I know I've done a lot of bad things, and I can't blame Malcolm for all of them. Still, I would never have hurt you or your daughter intentionally," Tania was vehement in her defense.

Lorelei didn't know if she believed the woman was especially sorry about taking her money. But something in her eyes said the latter part of her statement was genuine. "Why don't you tell me whatever it is you called me here to say?"

Tania nodded. "I couldn't be a party to any of it once I knew what he'd done."

She explained she'd only been the getaway driver the night of the fire. She hadn't even entered the building at all. "When Malcolm came running out, I could smell smoke on him, but I kept quiet. I only found out you'd been in the building with your little girl when I saw it on the news. They said he hit a guy over the head too, and I confronted him about everything, and he didn't even bother to deny any of it."

Lorelei took a slow breath, trying to regain her composure. It was one thing to suspect Malcolm had meant to hurt her, but it was another matter entirely when someone confirmed it. She looked at the woman who could barely meet her gaze. She noticed Tania was holding her sleeves down, despite the handcuffs. Lorelei reached out and pulled both sleeves up from the wrists. The woman had bruises, a lot of them, and probably not limited to her arms. "He did this to you?"

She nodded. "Doesn't matter, I deserve worse for everything I've put you through."

Lorelei didn't disagree with the woman. "Why was he searching my stuff? I took nothing of his when I left."

The woman paused, her confusion evident. "He never told me what he was looking for, only that he thought you had it or knew where it was. I think it might have been something belonging to your friend Ruby."

"I have hardly anything of hers either," Lorelei responded. All she had was a box of novels from the hospital, and they were in her storage locker.

"Like I said," Tania continued. "He didn't let me in on the full plan, just told me which parts I had to play, and I went along with it, until now."

Lorelei needed air and stood abruptly. She walked out of the room and headed for Coop's office again. Tania had imparted a slew of new information, but none of it was helping fill in the missing pieces. She was still pacing up and down when Coop walked in.

"I'm sorry Lorelei, I thought talking to her might help, but she doesn't seem to know much," he said.

"At least I know how she closed my bank account, she could easily pass for me," she said, and he nodded.

"She said there was one more thing she had to tell you. Are you ready to go back in there? If you feel there's no point, I'll take her back to the cell. She's being transferred to Arlington later this morning," he explained.

Lorelei didn't want to sit down opposite the woman again, but somewhere in the back of her mind, something was nagging at her, but she couldn't quite grasp it. It was enough to make her want to go back into the interrogation room to find out, she realized.

Tania Wilton was resting her forehead on the steel table. Her hands were still cuffed to the bar across the middle. She looked up as they walked back in, and in that split second of eye contact, Lorelei flashed back to where she'd seen the woman before. "Oh my God, it was you!" she felt the blood drain from her face. She was unsteady, nauseated, and dizzy all in the same moment.

"I'm sorry about that too," Tania closed her eyes.

Coop was looking from one to the other in confusion, and Lorelei wanted to enlighten him. Yet, as soon as she tried to speak, she hyperventilated. She didn't know why it was happening, but she couldn't stop it. Her breath was coming in shallow gasps, and in the middle of the anxiety attack, she realized she was crying. Tears poured down her cheeks as the woman looked embarrassed, and Coop looked about as uncomfortable as a man can.

"Why did you go along with any of it?" Lorelei finally choked the words out.

"I fell in love with him," Tania said. "When he's charming, he can get you to agree to pretty much anything, I think we both know that."

Lorelei nodded. "But why would he marry me just to get to Ruby?"

"Because he meant for me to be the one who got close to her, not you. I had been volunteering at the hospital for weeks when you arrived with your church group. You and Ruby just instantly bonded," she shrugged apologetically. "When he couldn't get to her that way, he came up with a plan to seduce you into marrying him."

Lorelei couldn't believe she had been so gullible. She'd fallen for Malcolm's lines because he was a skilled conman, and he'd charmed her. But there was one thing he wasn't, one *particularly important* thing, and it changed everything.

She felt tears clogging her throat again. "I have to get out of here," she mumbled, almost running from the room. She barely paused as she headed for the street, and even Coop's voice calling out to her had no effect.

It was chilly on Main Street, but she didn't care. She headed back towards Jefferson's house, hugging her arms across her body. Her jacket flapped in the breeze, but she didn't feel the cold. Her mind wouldn't stop racing, thought after thought tumbling through it, memories piecing together as she almost jogged up the street.

She'd been walking for a few minutes when she heard a vehicle heading her way at speed. When it did a U-turn and screeched to a halt a little ahead of her, she finally focused long enough to recognize Jefferson's new SUV.

He vaulted out of it and was standing right in front of her, holding her shoulders as he talked, but she couldn't seem to hear him. Why was that? She wondered. He was right there in front of her, but the roaring in her ears was deafening.

Her face was white, and tears were streaming down her cheeks, and Jefferson had never been more afraid in his life. "What happened, Lorelei?"

She didn't answer, and he got her into the front seat of his car and buckled her in before driving to Lake Thomas Park. He couldn't take her home to Beth and Madison in this emotional state, it would scare Beth out of her wits, and he had to admit to being pretty worried himself.

"Lorelei, I think you're in shock. What happened at the sheriff's office? Coop called me and said, you tore out of there after talking with the woman. Why Lorelei? Whatever it is, we can get through it together," he promised.

He parked way over in the back of the parking lot. No one was there this early on a Sunday morning, not when there was still a spring chill in the air, so they had the place to themselves. She unclipped her seat belt, and he wondered if she would get out of the car, but she climbed across to the driver's side and straddled his lap, resting her head on his shoulder.

"Lorelei, baby, tell me what the problem is, we'll fix it," he said.

She looked up, her eyes brimming with tears, then she smiled. She reached up and took Jefferson's face in her hands and pressed a tear dampened kiss on his lips. "I'm not married," was all she said before she kissed her way along his jaw to his collarbone.

"I don't understand," he said, trying to pay attention while his body stirred under hers.

"I was never married," she said.

Jefferson looked so baffled, and Lorelei couldn't blame him. This was like something straight out of a daytime soap. She took a breath, inhaling the clean scent that was essentially him. Then, she pressed another kiss on his throat, reveling in the fact that he could not keep his body from responding to hers, even though she was sure he was desperate for her to explain.

She sat back, staring into his eyes. "I'm sorry I lost it, I think I had so much pent up emotion, I couldn't keep it in any longer."

He reached out then and traced a finger over her lips. "You need to explain the *not* being married comment first."

"When I was talking to Tania Wilton, about her part in the whole scheme, I kept thinking she reminded me of someone. I mean, she does look enough like me to pass for my old driver's license photo," Lorelei began. "Suddenly I remembered I had seen her before, but her eyes were different and her hair. She was the woman in the law office the day I married Malcolm, except she was never a lawyer. Malcolm must have just rented the office to make the wedding look convincing."

She could see him processing the information, but he said nothing at all for what seemed like an eternity. "So, you're not married?"

She shook her head. "I never was, at least not to him, anyway. I have officially regained my widow status."

His eyes darkened then as he shifted his body under hers, and his gaze dropped to her lips. She knew what he was thinking because her mind was taking the same direction. When he reached between their bodies to rub between her legs, she moaned softly, and he pulled her flush against him. Their lips met, and his mouth ravaged hers unapologetically as their tongues tangled. Their hands explored under the clothing that suddenly seemed inconvenient.

He eased his power seat back as far as it would go, reclining it fully, pushing her jacket off, reaching for her sweater as she reached for his belt buckle. She was down to her tee-shirt and leggings, and he was out of his sweatshirt and bare-chested when they came up for air.

"I want you inside me," she told him boldly as she unzipped his pants and reached for him, finding him hard and ready.

She felt him lifting her, so he could slide down her leggings and underwear, neither of them caring they were about to have sex in his car in a public place. He positioned her over him and let her set the pace. It would be fast, she decided, because she needed him so much, and ever since that past Friday, all she'd wanted was to make love with him again.

His hands were under her shirt, pushing her bra out of the way so he could stroke her breasts, pinching her nipples lightly, causing her to clench her muscles around the length of him. He groaned as she squeezed him, and she did it repeatedly, delighting in the ripples of pleasure that had him thrusting deeper, harder, higher into her.

She knew she was on the brink of orgasm, and with a few gyrating motions of her hips, as she straddled him, she sent him tumbling over that precipice and joined him on his way back down to earth. She let her body collapse against his, catching her breath. "That was incredible," she whispered, trying not to move too much because he was still hard inside her.

"I've never had sex in a car before," Jefferson said, smiling like a thoroughly satisfied man. "I can see why teenagers do it."

"Me either. I think it gives the couch a run for its money," Lorelei joked.

He shook his head. "The couch was amazing, and so was this, but just wait until I get you back in my bed," he was sliding her displaced bra back into position as he spoke. He reached for her leggings, finally slipping out of her as he righted their clothing.

"We should get back," she said, more than a little reluctantly. "Who's there with the girls right now?"

He nodded as she scrambled back to the passenger seat. "Coop is there."

"Do you think he'll guess what we were up to?" Lorelei sent him a shy smile.

Jefferson shrugged. "He might, but, more importantly, can you find the energy right now to care because I can't."

Beth, Madison, and Coop were in the driveway playing basketball, although Jefferson didn't have a hoop. The aim seemed to be to get the ball past his brother and onto the front porch. Lorelei was sure Coop could have easily stopped them on more than one occasion, but the game was a way for them to get a little fresh air, which was never a bad thing for growing girls.

"Mom, you're home!" Beth rushed to her and almost tackled her to the ground.

"I missed you too," Lorelei laughed.

"You were gone for ages," her daughter admonished, and she knew she'd worried her.

"I have interesting news that was worth the wait," she promised, ushering the girls inside, leaving Jefferson outside to update Coop.

Once they were in the kitchen, both girls sat at the breakfast bar while she made them a snack. By the time she'd placed some cheesy crackers on a plate and gotten them some juice, Beth looked about ready to explode. "Mom, what is the news? Did they catch Malcolm? You cannot tell me something like that and then make me wait for so long!"

Lorelei burst out laughing, causing Beth to look at Madison in alarm. "Do you remember the day I married Malcolm in that law office?"

Beth faked gagging and glared at her, and Madison continued to look bemused.

"Do you remember the lady who married us?" She asked, and Beth nodded. "The lady in the lawyer's office is the same person as the one who closed out my bank accounts. I just met her at the sheriff's office. Her name is Tania Wilton, she was Malcolm's accomplice."

Madison still looked confused. "I don't understand what that means."

Beth looked askance at Lorelei, a hopeful gleam in her eyes. "Does that mean what I think it means?"

Lorelei nodded. "If you think it means that Malcolm and I were never really married, and it was all a big fake, then yes."

Beth shrieked with happiness. Then, she almost fell off her stool in her eagerness to reach her mother to give her another hug. The front door opened and closed, and Lorelei looked across the room, and her eyes locked with Jefferson's.

"I see your Mom told you the good news," he was smiling as broadly as Beth.

"Best Sunday ever!" Beth announced as she and Madison continued to dance around the kitchen island.

"Absolutely," Jefferson muttered, sliding his arms around Lorelei from behind as he reached the kitchen.

Lorelei hustled the two girls off to get ready for lunch at the Cooper's while remaining wrapped in Jefferson's embrace. As soon as they were alone, she turned in his arms, burying her face in his neck. "I can't believe what a crazy day this has been. I woke up thinking I was a married woman, wondering how long it would be before I could be free of him, and it turns out, I never was his."

Jefferson trailed kisses down her throat, stopping when he reached her collarbone. "I say we agree to never have a weekend quite like this one again, apart from certain aspects," he murmured provocatively.

Amen to that, Lorelei thought. "I forgot to ask before, how is Jackson? Is he going to leave the hospital today?"

"They discharged him already. He's at my Dad's. He's a little sore still, but he will be fine," he said, and she felt tears clogging her throat again. "Hey, no need to cry, I told you everything would be all right, and boy, did I hit that one out of the park!"

This man, Lorelei thought happily, is the forever kind of love I never thought I'd find again. "I love you so much, Jefferson," she whispered as she brought her lips up to his and kissed him tenderly. She felt him freeze as she pulled back, and he looked dumbfounded. "What's wrong?"

He smiled that toe-curling sexy-as-all-hell smile he reserved just for her, and she realized why: she'd never said those words to him out loud before, even though she'd known she was in love with him for quite some time. "I'm sorry I didn't say it when you did. I should have, I felt it too, but I was a little overwhelmed at the time."

"It's okay, Lorelei I knew it in my heart anyway, you have the world's worst poker face," he tilted his head and kissed a path down to that sweet spot beneath her ear that always drove her crazy.

"Mom, can I take my iPad with me? I want to show Madison what I built in Minecraft," Beth called from the guest room.

Jefferson groaned and stepped back, putting some space between them for the sake of his sanity. "I'll let you wrangle those two while I go start the car."

Lorelei smiled, touching his cheek softly before moving away, and he knew he'd found the kind of love his parents had shared. He'd never understood how someone could say it felt like their heart was full, but he did now. He was sure his brothers would know as soon as they saw him. They would be relentless in reminding him he'd vowed never to let a woman get under his skin again after Stephanie. But Lorelei was not merely under his skin, she was his *everything*. Her smile made his world brighter, her tears made him want to slay dragons for her, her daughter made him long for the day they would welcome siblings for her into the world.

It was only as he started the car that he finally admitted to himself what he wanted from Lorelei; he wanted till death do us part. He wanted her in a white dress and him in a tuxedo. He wanted two cute ten-year-old girls throwing rose petals. But mostly, he wanted Lorelei in his life, in his bed, in his corner, by his side, forever. The woman in question opened the passenger side door then and stepped up into the SUV, giving him a questioning look. "Are you feeling okay? You look like you want to be sick or something."

He managed a smile for her and for the two little girls buckling up in the back seat. "I'm just tired, it's been an eventful weekend," he said, unable to resist teasing her a little and loving the way she blushed right on cue for him.

When they pulled into the driveway of his Dad's house, Jefferson saw Grace looking out, as if she were waiting for them to arrive. They were almost at the front door when it opened, and his sister ran out and threw her arms around Lorelei. "You're not married! That is the best news I've ever heard!"

"You told them," Jefferson asked Coop as they made their way inside.

Coop nodded and grinned. "I bet that development made you all kinds of happy."

He didn't know what came over him, but he engulfed his older brother in a hug, then he saw Jackson heading over to them, and everything hit him at once. He broke free of Coop, and when Jackson wrapped his arms around him, they held on tight. Jefferson pulled back first. "You ever scare me like that again, I'll kick your ass."

A knock at the front door revealed Daniel and Toby. Madison squealed and ran over to her father to tell him the news, and the male bonding fest was over, much to Jefferson's relief. Everyone seemed to talk at once, and he looked over at Lorelei. She smiled happily back at him and mouthed, *are you okay?* He nodded and jerked his head toward the back door.

"Where are you two going?" Harry Cooper growled as they walked through the kitchen. Jefferson looked back over his shoulder and met his father's narrowed eyes. "We need to get a little fresh air." His father raised his eyebrows but didn't say a word.

They were still wearing their coats as they walked into the gazebo. When they reached the center of the octagonal structure, Jefferson paused, turning Lorelei to face him. "I love you with all my heart and soul, Lorelei."

Her eyes misted as she reached up to cup his face in her hands. "I feel the same way about you, Jefferson, you know that. I've never loved any man as much as I love you."

He knew it, which was why he took a step backward and, nervously, dropped onto one knee.

Lorelei's eyes widened in shock. She heard hollers and cheers from inside the house. Was this really happening? She thought giddily.

"I don't have a ring to give you, but there will be one, but I don't want to wait another day to ask you because I know you're the woman I want to spend the rest of my life loving," he paused. "Lorelei Hannah, will you be my wife?" She could tell he was holding his breath. He had to be almost positive that he knew what her answer would be, but his uncertainty was endearingly sweet.

Joyfully, she wrapped her arms around his neck, almost knocking him over in his kneeling position. Tears were streaming unchecked down her cheeks as she nodded her assent and kissed him. She vaguely heard more cheering coming from the house, but they had more important things to do than acknowledge the catcalls. When they came up for air, the door opened, and everyone spilled onto the deck.

Beth rushed up to wrap her arms around them. "I can't wait for us to be a proper family!"

"We already are," Harry Cooper grinned. "And I got my first grandchild!"

"She's my granddaughter too!" Toby announced. "I got dibs on that."

Daniel stepped forward then and shook hands with Jefferson before pulling her into a hug. "This time I want to be at the wedding," he said firmly.

She smiled again, knowing her face would hurt later from all the happiness she was feeling, but she didn't care. "I was hoping you would be the one to give me away," she said, and Daniel nodded readily.

"And when is this wedding going to be happening?" Toby asked, his Irish slipping out as he hugged her next.

"June," Jefferson answered.

Lorelei looked around at him in shock. "You do realize that's only a few weeks away." He raised an eyebrow, cocking his head on one side. "You're serious?"

"I'd marry you today if I could, but you deserve the white dress, bridesmaids, the whole shebang," he said.

"Maybe we could get married here, in the gazebo?" Lorelei mused.

Madison and Beth jumped up and down in excitement, and Harry Cooper smiled, puffing out his chest in pride. "Give me a few weeks to get the yard looking perfect, and you have a deal!"

Everyone filed back inside then, leaving Lorelei and Jefferson standing alone in the gazebo. "Are you sure you want to do this so fast?" she asked.

Jefferson slid his arms around her waist and pulled her close. "Absolutely. Why would I want to wait when I know I found the only woman for me? I love you so much, Lorelei, and if she's agreeable, I want to adopt Beth too."

"I think she would love that," Lorelei whispered. "Thank you for stopping for us that snowy day in March, Jefferson. I'm glad I didn't get in your car now because maybe all this wouldn't have happened if I had," she said, but he shook his head. "You think we would still be here either way?" she asked.

"Ruby sent you here to us. I never believed in fate or any of that before. Still, you two had to meet and become friends for any of this to happen. So, yeah, we were always going to be together, one way or the other," he said, dropping a kiss on her forehead. "Now let's go eat before the hordes descend on us again.

EPILOGUE

Lorelei had never known six weeks could pass so slowly and yet seem to have flown by. There was so much to do to get ready for the wedding, but they had pulled the entire thing together so well. She'd also taken a position on the reception desk at the new spa and started right after the honeymoon. She'd done her fair share of work at the festival too. Even the repairs to Toby's building were going well. However, Cooper Law was still operating out of Jefferson's living room right now.

She'd found her perfect wedding dress and taken all her furniture out of storage to move it into Jefferson's garage. The last few weeks had been more than a little overwhelming, but finally, their big day had arrived, the day she would become Mrs. Cooper. She was more than a little nervous standing in the middle of Grace's bedroom in her robe, waiting for her maid of honor to return, but she felt happy.

Grace came back into the room, still wearing a bathrobe herself because she wanted to wait until the last minute to put on her pale rose-colored dress. Madison and Beth had been so excited they'd been up since before dawn. They were waiting in the family room for Lorelei to come downstairs, already wearing their dresses. Lorelei watched as Jefferson's sister stepped quickly into her bridesmaid dress, then pulled the zipper up for her. "You look beautiful, Grace."

"Thank you, Lorelei. Are you ready for your dress now?" Grace asked, looking misty-eyed.

"I'm *so* ready," Lorelei laughed as Grace helped her step into the off-white three-quarter length dress. It zipped without a problem, and she breathed a sigh of relief. She had one more surprise for Jefferson, something that had most definitely not been on the to-do list, but she was sure he would be happy about it. Unconsciously, she covered her stomach as she looked in the mirror and saw Grace's eyes widen.

"Are you…?"

"I am. I took three tests because I couldn't believe it myself," Lorelei said as Grace hugged her tightly.

"We can't ruin our mascara, but Lorelei, I am so happy for you both," Grace said. "My brother has never been more content than he has since he met you."

Someone knocked on the bedroom door, and Daniel's voice came from outside. "Are you decent in there?"

"You can come in Daniel, I'm almost ready to go," Lorelei said, blinking away the tears Grace's words had evoked.

"Is everything okay?" he asked, looking from one to the other.

"We are absolutely fine," Grace said. "But I should go now, let you have a minute. I need to make sure the girls are ready. Excuse me."

Grace almost ran out of the room, and Lorelei laughed much to Daniel's consternation. "I don't know how many more ways I can tell her she did not offend me by what she said that night," Daniel said gruffly.

It was only then that Lorelei saw the package in his hands. "You didn't have to bring me a gift," she joked. He held out the padded envelope, and the seriousness in his blue eyes gave her pause. She took the package and looked at it. It was addressed to her, and she knew the handwriting well; it belonged to Ruby. "I don't understand?" she murmured. "How can this be?"

"When I was checking out some leads on Malcolm last week, I called at your old apartment building, and the office had been holding a package for you. You didn't leave a forwarding address, and there wasn't a return address, so they put it in a drawer and forgot about it," Daniel explained.

"I forwarded my mail through the post office, maybe the package came the day we left?" Lorelei mused.

"I didn't know whether I should bring it today, but I thought maybe it was what Malcolm was looking for," Daniel said.

Lorelei's eyes went wide with anticipation. Here goes nothing! She thought. She ripped across the top and looked inside the envelope, and there it was, Ruby's journal, the one she had carried everywhere with her. A rubber band was around it, and there was a note attached. She read it aloud.

Lorelei,

This is my last journal, please read it and tell my family I never stopped loving them.

Your friend, Ruby.

Removing the band, Lorelei opened the journal, and several photos slid to the floor.

"I'll get them," Daniel said, and as he picked up the pictures, she saw him pause.

"What is it?" she asked, taking the photos from his hand. "Oh, my."

A young Ruby stood in one photo, with her parents by her side. Toby looked so young, Lorelei thought. Another shot was of Ruby alone, probably around the age she had run away. The next one showed her with a small boy holding her hand and a baby in her arms. Lorelei looked at the inscription on the first page of the journal then and read it sadly. *For my children and my parents. I'm sorry.*

The first page began with Ruby writing about her cancer diagnosis and how her treatment was going. The date at the top of the page showed it as being a few months before Lorelei had first met her. Lorelei stopped reading. "I think it's her life story or part of it. I can't believe she has children out there somewhere, and Toby has grandkids. But we can't tell him about this yet, not until we can find out more."

Daniel looked as surprised as she felt and didn't seem to know what to say either. "Can you hold on to this until I get back from my honeymoon? I don't want to leave it at home, but I definitely don't want to take it with me to the Caribbean, either?"

"You know I'll take care of it," Daniel assured her. "Would you mind if I read some of it? Maybe there are clues in it about Malcolm. I'm sure this is what he was searching for when he set fire to your apartment. There has to be something in here that he wants."

"I think there might be more journals somewhere too, but I don't have them," Lorelei murmured. "You don't think Malcolm could be the little boy in the photo, do you?"

Daniel shrugged. "Maybe, but I thought he was older than you?"

Lorelei shrugged. "If he told the truth about that, he was about five years older than me."

"Well, if he wasn't lying about his age, then he'd be too old based on when Ruby disappeared. He wanted something from her for sure, we just don't know what that was yet, but we will," Daniel was sure.

"Well, you should hold on to this for safekeeping then because I need to get downstairs. I'm getting married today," Lorelei giggled a little as she handed him the leather-bound journal. Her nerves were resurfacing as she covered her cheeks with her palms. "Oh my gosh, I'm getting married today!"

"You sure are!" Daniel grinned. "Are you ready to go?"

"Absolutely!" she said, slipping her feet into the highest backless heels she had found at the bridal store. Today she would be as tall as she could be for Jefferson for that first wedded kiss.

Jefferson paced beside the gazebo, and around the gazebo and even in it. He knew Lorelei was upstairs still because Grace had told him Daniel Sullivan was with her. He wasn't nervous about Danny being with her; it wasn't even really that at all. He just wanted the ceremony to be over and the party to begin because then she would be his wife. His brothers kept grinning at him and making jokes about him having pre-wedding jitters, but even their ribbing wasn't getting to him. "You wait until this happens to you; you won't be so smug then."

"We're not smug," Jackson said, smiling. "And we can both see why you've fallen for her so hard, she's the yin to your yang."

"Places everyone," Harry Cooper called, stepping out of the kitchen onto the silk-draped gazebo. "The bride is on her way!"

It had stunned Jefferson when his father announced he was performing the ceremony. He'd become ordained online specifically for the occasion. They had set chairs up on the back lawn for the guests to sit in, but there were only about forty of them because they'd both wanted to keep the celebration intimate. The white carpeted aisle led around the side of the house to the steps of the gazebo, and everyone stood as the wedding march played through the outdoor sound system.

Madison and Beth walked together. They were holding baskets of pink rose petals, and they dropped them delicately onto the white carpet as they proceeded down the aisle. Grace followed behind with Coop on her arm. He was wearing a black tuxedo instead of his standard uniform, and she wore a simple rose-colored vee neck A-line dress that brushed her calves.

"Here she comes," Jackson whispered in Jefferson's ear as Lorelei came into sight. Her smile bright enough to light up Northern Virginia. "Wow."

Wow, indeed, Jefferson thought. His wife-to-be looked ethereal. Her understated beauty making him catch his breath as he watched her walking on the arm of Daniel Sullivan. Daniel didn't seem wholly unaffected by the occasion, either. He guided Lorelei carefully down the aisle and held out her hand for Jefferson to take as she walked up the steps.

He smiled, seeing the heels she was wearing and the concentration on her face. "You don't have to wear those for me, I love how petite you are," he whispered in her ear as they turned to face his father, but she shot him a determined look that said the shoes were staying on.

The photographer they'd chosen was clicking away in the background as his father spoke of love, loyalty, and family. When it came time for him to say his vows, he didn't even take out the piece of paper he'd written them on because he didn't need to. "Lorelei, I promise to love you, honor you, and protect you and our family till death do us part. You are my heart Lorelei, I will love you forever," he stopped and saw tears welling in her eyes. He hadn't meant to make her cry, but then, he knew he had tears in his eyes too.

"Jefferson, I will always love you. You stole my heart so fast I could barely believe it was real. I found peace and love in your arms, and I plan on spending the rest of my life there, with you and our children," she smiled and waited. There was something in the way she said it and something in the way her eyes were twinkling up at him.

He leaned in close to her ear, almost holding his breath before he spoke. "Are you trying to tell me something?" She didn't respond, but the impish giggle that escaped her lips was answer enough. He swept her up in his arms, kissing her as he twirled her around in the gazebo, much to the consternation of his Dad.

"Hey, I'm not finished yet!" Harry said, speaking the final words of the ceremony over the cheers of the guests.

"Do I even need to say you may kiss the bride?" he asked ironically. Jefferson and Lorelei finally broke apart. Beth rushed up to them, and they shared their happy news with her as the photographer's shutter clicked away continuously, capturing every moment of their joy.

"Can we tell everyone else?" He whispered in her ear, hoping she would say yes because he wanted to shout it from the rooftops, and Beth was nodding eagerly. When she consented, he turned to their guests. "My wife and I are having a baby!"

The gathering erupted in cheers, and as Lorelei took in the scene from her lofty spot in the gazebo, alongside her new husband, she knew she had found her forever home.

Coming Soon

Grace & Daniel's story

Join my mailing list for updates and more:

www.candyyork.com

Made in the USA
Middletown, DE
01 October 2020

20915949R00130